WENDY PERCIVAL was bor[...] brought up in the Worcestersh[...] as a primary school teacher [...] in 1980 to take up her first t[...] teaching for twenty years.

An impulse buy of *Writing Magazine* inspired her to start writing seriously. She won *Writing Magazine*'s Summer Ghost Story competition in 2002 and had a short story published in *The People's Friend* before focusing on full-length fiction.

The time honoured 'box of old documents in the attic' stirred her interest in genealogy and became the inspiration for the Esme Quentin Mysteries – *Blood-Tied*, *The Indelible Stain* and *The Malice of Angels*.

When she's not writing fiction, Wendy conducts her own family history research, sharing her finds on her blog, www.familyhistorysecrets.blogspot.com. She's also had articles published in Shropshire Family History Society's quarterly journal and in *Family Tree* magazine.

Wendy lives in a thatched cottage beside a thirteenth-century church with her husband and a particularly talkative cat.

You can find more on her website wendypercival.co.uk.

Death
of a
Cuckoo

WENDY
PERCIVAL

SilverWood

Originally published in 2017 as an ebook by sBooks
an imprint of SilverWood Books Ltd

This paperback edition published by SilverWood Books 2017

SilverWood Books Ltd
14 Small Street, Bristol, BS1 1DE, United Kingdom
www.silverwoodbooks.co.uk

ISBN 978-1-78132-738-8 (paperback)
ISBN 978-1-78132-649-7 (sBooks ebook)

British Library Cataloguing in Publication Data
A CIP catalogue record for this book is available from
the British Library

Page design and typesetting by SilverWood Books
Printed on responsibly sourced paper

1

Strange how an innocent-looking photograph can be so explosive. Two young women, laughing into the camera, raising their glasses in celebration of a national event, without the slightest clue of the impact their image would have some thirty years later.

The disturbing truth churned around my head like a river in spate as I sat on my late mum's patio in the weak February sunshine. The lawn, on which I'd played as a child, had grown long over the mild winter months and needed attention. I gazed at the old apple tree by the fence with its low bough where I used to climb and sit, swinging my legs and looking out at the world beyond the garden fence. It seemed so long ago, in a different world. A world which was now crumbling around me.

I laid down the offending photograph on top of Carol's sympathy card and accompanying letter of condolence and hugged my coat around me. I should contact this woman, this apparent long-lost friend of my mum's and tell her she'd made a mistake. Except she hadn't, of course. How could she? The letter said everything. *Dear Gina, I'm so sorry,* she'd written. But her regret was at Mum's passing and their loss of contact over the years. She could have no notion of the turmoil her photograph would create, the confusion her knowledge would cause. And I had no idea what to do.

I rubbed my eyes, letting my head slump forward so that my hair hung down over my face. In reality, I didn't actually have to *do* anything. I could push the matter to one side, dismiss it as an anomaly. I had plenty else to occupy me without dwelling on false testimony by some woman I didn't even know. This now redundant family home needed sorting, its unwanted contents cleared and disposed of. My parents had lived here since before I was born; it was going to take a lot longer than a few hours over a couple of wet weekends. I just needed to get on with it.

I could start with something simple. The rest of today's post, perhaps. More condolence cards to add to those in the living room from people like Carol, who'd heard the news on the grapevine rather than from me, as they weren't in Mum's address book.

But the nagging question remained. How could I ignore the truth?

The thought triggered a fresh welling of tears. I sniffed and blinked them away. I didn't have a choice, did I? I had to deal with it, and that meant looking for the evidence to confirm her claim. And force me to confront the truth.

I stood up and headed for the back door. The office. That's where my parents kept official documents. If any paperwork existed to back up Carol's words, that's where I'd find it.

I yanked open the back door and stopped abruptly. Someone was moving around inside the house. I paused on the threshold to listen. A trapped bird, perhaps? No. This was no panicked fluttering of wings. This was human. The distinct sound of a filing cabinet drawer clamming shut confirmed it. Someone was in the office.

Fighting the overwhelming urge to flee screaming back into the garden, I forced myself to creep across the kitchen and into the hall. The office door was ajar. Muted shadows flickered in the narrow opening as the intruder moved erratically around the room.

I stood in the hall, inert with fear and indecision. Should I peer inside with the hope of identifying my uninvited visitor? Burst in and demand to know what was going on? Or retreat and telephone the police?

The latter option might be the safest but unless a patrol car was parked within a hundred metres of the front door – unlikely – I'd be wasting my time. I felt too fragile for a confrontation. Which left me with only one choice. Holding my breath, I reached out and gently pushed open the door with my fingertips.

I'd forgotten the bloody door creaked. I flinched. The

intruder looked up in alarm, eyes wide and bloodshot. I shrieked and backed away into the hall, as he came at me. He shoved me aside and pushed past. I stumbled backwards against the door of the under-stairs cupboard and crashed to the floor. I heard the front door open and he was gone.

I curled up into a foetal position and sobbed.

2

I lay listless on the hall carpet, exhausted and with my head throbbing. This, I told myself in the sternest tone I could muster, would simply not do. I pulled myself into a sitting position and slumped against the wall, sniffing and wiping my hands across my face. I was not a child. Get a grip, for God's sake.

I picked myself up off the floor and hobbled to the front door, which gaped open to the chill of the morning. I pushed my hair off my face and peered out, checking up and down the street. But, of course, my intruder had long gone. I cursed myself at not having more bottle and demanding to know what he was doing in Mum's house. I slammed the door closed with a force which reverberated down the hall.

I returned to the room which my parents had referred to, in the early days, as the library. It boasted two walls of books on floor-to-ceiling shelves and a small, tatty leather chair, which once belonged to Dad's grandfather, sat in the corner for quiet contemplation and reading. But the chair hadn't been used as intended since Dad died five years ago and so the room, dominated as it was now by a modern desk, a computer table and an unnecessarily large filing cabinet, had become the office.

I picked up the telephone to call the police, recalling the man's gaunt face and unkempt, greasy hair, ready to give them a description, while scanning the room for anything missing. They'd be sure to ask.

Had he been looking for cash? Perhaps he'd heard the place was empty. It seemed odd to me that he was searching the filing cabinet. Wouldn't he head for the bedroom for jewellery? Unless he was after something else. Documents? Papers? What could be of value in my mum's filing cabinet? Nothing I knew of.

I went over and pulled open the top drawer. There were no files out of place, no gaps in evidence of where he'd searched. I slammed it shut and tried the next drawer down. Nothing there. The bottom drawer gave no clues, either. I suppose it was a place people might keep a cash box. Maybe he'd struck lucky in the past.

I dropped down on the leather chair, suddenly spent. It occurred to me that if he'd taken anything, I'd have seen it as he'd run away. He'd shoved me aside so forcefully; he must have been empty handed.

My gaze fell on the desk. Mum's weekly appointment diary lay open and discarded on the heap of today's post. I was sure it hadn't been like that earlier.

I got up and went across to the desk and picked up the diary, open at a date two weeks ago. There was the visit to her hairdresser that she'd never keep, which I'd cancelled having found the salon appointment card pinned to the kitchen corkboard after she died. The only other entry was on the following day, where she'd written a single letter J. Who or what was J?

I flicked through the previous pages. The letter J appeared regularly.

I shrugged. So what? I could think of at least two of her friends with a name beginning with J. Janet and Joan. Presumably it was enough for Mum to know which one she was meeting. No point in reading anything into it.

I turned back to the handset, my finger hovering over the keypad. So what was the number you dialled these days to report an incident to the police? 101? 111? Or was that the NHS?

Oh, this was ridiculous. Did I really need to involve the police? Nothing had been stolen. No harm done. They had plenty of serious crimes to deal with. They didn't need my something-or-nothing burglary cluttering up their workload. Besides, I wasn't convinced I was in any fit state to answer their inevitable questions.

Questions. The word jolted me like stab in the back. I'd been on my way to find an answer to the question Carol's letter and photograph had raised.

I knelt down beside the desk and opened the cupboard

at the rear of the kneehole. Inside was an old wooden box in which Dad had kept legal documents. I knew what to look for and, however hard it would be, I had to know.

I dragged the box out of the cupboard and sat down on the floor, my heart pounding so hard I thought it might burst my eardrums. With shaking hands, I flicked through the papers until I came across something unfamiliar. I put the box aside and, forcing down the panic rising in my throat, I took a deep breath, opened it out and read it.

But clarification eluded me. Instead what I saw compounded my confusion and only added to my growing anguish.

3

The lady in the library assured me Esme Quentin came highly recommended and with all the skills needed to advise me. Her profile formed part of a display by the local family history society, advertising for new members to research their genealogical past. One testimonial from a former client paid tribute to Mrs Quentin's ability to "break down brick walls". I desperately hoped she could do the same for me.

When I contacted her to make the arrangements I gave little away. I still found my dilemma difficult to put into words, even wondering whether I'd be capable of explaining how I needed her help. Perhaps if it would be easier simply to show her everything and let her deduce what I wanted from her. It was her field, after all.

I decided we should meet at Mum's house, rather than mine. It seemed appropriate, given that Mum and everything that the family home implied was at the centre of my troubles. In the hours leading up to the meeting the enormity of what I was facing seemed almost overwhelming. I'd bitten my nails down to ground zero by the time the doorbell rang. I took a deep breath, wiped my damp palms on the thighs of my jeans and answered the door.

A woman in a red duffel coat with hair the colour of Cornish sand looked back at me from the front step, a large canvas bag slung over her shoulder. 'Gina Vincent?' she said, tipping her head to one side.

I nodded. 'You must be Esme. Come on in.' I stood back to let her pass. She was shorter than me and much older – late forties, early fifties at a guess – and wore her hair up in a clip at the back of her head. But what was impossible to ignore was the ragged scar across her cheek.

I dragged my gaze away and gestured towards the front room. We made the usual remarks about the weather as she took off her coat. She was dressed in a jade calf-length skirt and a plain sweater, a scarf in swirling green shades draped around her neck.

'Thanks for coming so promptly,' I said.

She scrutinised me. 'You did sound a bit...'

'Desperate?' I offered.

She smiled. 'Let's just say I sensed your urgency.' She sat down on the sofa and looked around at the array of cards on the mantle-piece. 'Oh, my condolences. I didn't realise. Your...?'

'Mum.' I flushed, embarrassed at not having prepared her. 'Sorry. I should have said. Truth is I don't know

14

whether I'm coming or going. Since she died...well, I've stumbled across...which is why...' I put my hand to my head. 'Hey, what am thinking? I haven't even offered you a drink.'

Esme shook her head. 'No, I'm fine. Look, why not sit down and fill me in?'

Her tone was warm and I slid into the armchair seat, comforted by her encouragement.

But now it came to it, where to begin? The letter? The photograph? The confusing document? I blinked, unable to form the first sentence.

'You said something about a genealogical conundrum,' Esme prompted.

'Yes, but it's all such a mess. I don't know where to start.'

Esme leaned forward and gave me an encouraging smile. 'From the beginning is usually the best place. Tell me about your mum.'

I nodded and took a deep breath. I told her about being called to the hospital, about Mum's fatal heart attack, about the shock of finding myself alone in the world. I told her about my discovery of something which had blown my world apart. And I told her about the intruder.

She gasped. 'Oh, no. You poor girl. How terrifying.'

'Like I really needed that as well,' I said, forcing a half laugh. 'I couldn't believe it.'

'I'm sure you couldn't. Dreadful. What did the police

say?' She must have seen something in my face as her expression changed. 'You have reported it, I hope?'

I shook my head. 'I was going to but I didn't bother in the end. What would I say? Nothing's been stolen. I couldn't see the point?'

'You'd at least have access to victim support. That might help.'

I batted her suggestion away. 'I just don't need the hassle.' I stood up. 'Look, why don't I stop offloading on you and get to the point of why I asked you here?' I fetched Carol's incriminating photograph from the sideboard and handed it to her. She dug in her bag for a pair of glasses before taking the photo and studying it.

'The woman on the left with long dark hair like mine is my mum,' I said. 'The blonde is someone called Carol. She wrote to me, having heard about Mum, and in her letter she told me something which...' I swallowed. '...well, it's completely thrown me.'

Esme took off her reading glasses and regarded me with concern. 'Go on.'

'I hadn't contacted her to let her know what had happened because, well, I didn't know anything about her. Her name certainly isn't in Mum's address book and, according to Carol, that's 'cos she and Mum lost touch. They'd met while they were in hospital years ago and supported one another afterwards. Mum had a hysterectomy, you see. It's why I don't have any brothers and sisters.

She and Carol were going through similar traumas and had their operations at the same time.' I let out a shaky breath. It was harder than I'd imagined to voice the disturbing facts out loud. I nodded towards the photograph. 'Mum and Carol met in hospital the year that photo was taken, which, as you can see from the banner at the back, was when Charles and Diana got married.'

'Which was, what? 1981?'

'Yes.' I swallowed. 'Which means,' I said, fighting back the sob rising in my throat, 'that Mum could never have given birth to me, because I was born in 1984, three years after her operation.'

4

I stood up and paced the room, giving Esme time to absorb the implications. She rubbed a forefinger along the scar on her cheek, prompting me to wonder about the injury. A car accident? A childhood incident? Did she ever talk about it?

'You're sure about the dates?' Esme said, after a while.

'You've seen the photograph. And Carol's letter's quite clear. They got to know one another on the ward. The celebration in the picture was sometime afterwards.' I sat down on the edge of the chair and leaned over. 'She said in her letter how glad she was that Mum had been able to adopt. There's no question about it.'

Esme nibbled the edge of her thumbnail. 'So I assume now this is about finding your birth mother? I'm wondering whether you'd be better speaking to someone who specialises in this sort of thing. It's not my field of expertise.'

I held up my hand. 'Hear me out. This isn't what you think.'

Esme frowned. 'OK. I'm listening.'

I sat down again and linked my fingers together. 'After everything Carol had said, I was a mess. I didn't want to believe it.'

'I can understand that.'

I looked down at my hands. 'Still don't. I mean, how could my parents not tell me?'

'It's not unheard of, Gina, though perhaps not as much in these more enlightened days.'

'Maybe. The thing is the only birth certificate I've ever had is one of those something-or-nothing ones, you know. Just my name, place and date of birth.'

'The short version, without the parents' details.'

I nodded. 'I've never had a proper one. So, when I came to think about it, it all added up. Carol must be right – I was adopted. Which I'd never know from the birth certificate I've always used, which is why my parents were able to keep me in the dark. But I reckoned somewhere must be my adoption papers. So I went to search for them.'

'To use them to get a copy of your original birth certificate and hence the name of your biological mother.'

'That was the plan, yes.' I stood up again and fetched a white envelope from off the sideboard. 'Interestingly, Carol said she was really sorry that after I'd come along she and Mum had lost touch.'

Esme shrugged. 'It happens. Busy lives, especially where children are involved.'

'Except Carol felt Mum had deliberately cut off ties between them.'

'Did she say why?'

'I think it was because she had something to hide.' I handed her the envelope. 'You might think so too when you read this.'

Esme took the envelope and drew out the document inside. I watched as she read through the information – Gina Vincent, born 14th June 1984 at Hawks Hall, Exmoor. Father's name Stuart Vincent, mother's name Andrea Vincent, formerly Newby.

Esme took off her reading glasses and looked up. 'But this is your full birth certificate,' she said, puzzled.

'Except it isn't, is it?' I folded my arms. 'Because we both know that everything on that document is a lie.'

5

Esme sat back in her seat and for a moment said nothing. I could see she was intrigued but was she working out how to break it to me there was nothing she could do, that the past would have to remain a mystery.

'I know adopted children have the right to see their original certificate,' I said, unable to keep quiet any longer. 'Which, if they're lucky, ultimately leads them to their real mother. But this *is* ostensibly my original birth certificate. End of the line.'

Esme took a breath and let it out slowly through pursed lips. 'You're right in calling it a conundrum, I'll say that.'

'Well?' I prompted. 'What do you think? Will you help? I wouldn't know where to start and, without any adoption paperwork to go on, neither would any of your experts.' I let out an exasperated sigh. 'It's why I came to you. I heard Esme Quentin was someone who saw the impossible as a challenge.'

Esme gave me a wry smile. 'Who told you that?'

'You will help, won't you?'

Esme leaned forward and rested her elbow on the arm of the sofa. She looked at me intently, a serious expression on her face. 'Gina, you have to understand that if we do this, you're taking a risk. You don't know what you're going to find. "Be careful what you wish for" might be a phrase banded around a lot these days, but it makes a serious point.'

'And you don't think what I've discovered already isn't painful?' I said, feeling my face redden. 'You can't opt out just because it might be uncomfortable?'

Her face softened. 'Gina, I'm not saying that. Neither am I declining my help. But you have to accept that what I uncover...what *we* uncover might be more than you bargained for. I don't want you to take that route without being sure it's what you want. That's all I'm saying. You have to be prepared.'

I flicked my hair behind my shoulders. 'The truth doesn't scare me, Esme,' I said. 'I can handle it, whatever we find. At least I'd know, then. For sure. It's got to be better than my imagination in overdrive. I mean, how bad can it be?'

*

Despite my bullish declaration that I could cope with whatever came to light, the level of trepidation heightened as Esme left the house. She gave me two days to think about things, after which time I was to let her know my decision. She wouldn't start anything until she heard from me.

After she'd gone, I wondered whether she'd seen something in my manner suggesting I may not cope with whatever she might find. Was that why she was hesitant about taking the job? Or did she issue the same caution to all of her clients?

I had an urge to be back in my own home. I grabbed my keys and went out of the front door, slamming it behind me. As I climbed into the driver's seat of my car, I examined the idea of pushing aside the questions my birth certificate had raised and simply concluding that it was some sort of administrative error. After all, what difference did it make? I might never had known had Carol not got in touch and thrown the innocent, yet explosive, comment into the conversation. I could be coming to terms with my mum's death, sailing the emotional waters of the loss of a parent, much as everyone else might. Dealing with paperwork, clearing a house that had once been a home, crying over old photographs of childhood memories but knowing that it was part of an order where life continued, moving the generations on.

But that was the whole point, wasn't it? All those childhood memories and certainties were now tainted, weren't they? The foundations on which they were built were found to be faulty. But in what way? What was the story behind my birth? Why the lie? What was the real reason why Mum had severed ties with Carol?

I slammed the heel of my hand against the steering

wheel. It wasn't fair. Why had I never been told? Like many on learning they'd been adopted, I should have had the chance to protest to my adoptive parents. But I'd never had the satisfaction of being able to rant on about the trauma and injustice of where I found myself, while someone offered reassurance by putting the opposing view and, in the end, convincing me that while everything had changed, nothing had changed and my parents remained the people who loved, cared for me and continued to do so.

I squeezed my eyes shut. And wasn't withholding the truth done with the child's interest at heart, a misbelief that the knowledge that their parents weren't their own flesh and blood might make them feel less loved? Was that what had happened here? Had my parents kept the true circumstances from me to protect me? Shouldn't I accept that fact, then, and move on?

I opened my eyes and looked out on to the street. A mother was strapping a toddler into his car seat at the house opposite. A father was striding along the pavement hand in hand with his daughter who was skipping along beside him. An elderly man shuffled along with a shopping bag, passing the time of day with the father and daughter. All getting on with the ordinariness of life. Was there any reason why I couldn't do the same?

Because I'd always wonder. A chance remark, a TV drama, the lyrics of a song. Anything might plant the question back in my path. And I'd experience the same shock every time it happened, I'm sure I would. No. I had to do this. I had to find out, however long it took, or the unknown truth would forever fester. And who knows what worse damage that might do.

I reached for the ignition and started the car. My mind was made up. I'd let Esme know my decision in the morning. I only hoped I had the courage to see it through, whatever the truth proved to be.

6

Esme phoned three days later. She said she had something to show me. We arranged to meet in a cafe in town. I saw her sitting at a table in the window as I arrived. She waved when she saw me and gave me a reassuring smile. When we'd spoken on the phone she'd suggested the most obvious place to start our search was the place in Devon where, supposedly, I'd been born. Given the circumstances, Esme felt it may be significant that I'd been born in Devon when my parents lived in Shropshire. As far as I'd been told, Mum had gone into labour when they were on holiday, hence my birth being registered in Barnstaple, which I'd assumed to have been in the district hospital. I was even more convinced now that my parents had deliberately avoided admitting that I had a full birth certificate so I had no reason to ask awkward questions.

I pushed open the door to the cafe, squeezed past a large woman with enough shopping bags to fill a skip and sat down with some sense of trepidation.

'Don't look so terrified,' Esme said. 'I'm just gathering

background information for the moment.'

'Oh, OK,' I swallowed. 'What sort of background information?'

'About Hawks Hall, the Devon address mentioned on your birth certificate.' She slid a photograph across the table. 'It's right on the edge of Exmoor, about a mile or so outside a village called Westford. Someone's suggested to me that at the time you were born it was a private hospital.'

I pulled the photograph towards me for a closer look. It was a large austere house with tall windows and lofty chimneys. The rendered walls were stained with grime and several windows had been boarded up. If I expected to feel any sort of affinity with the place, I didn't. My overwhelming emotion was distaste. It looked cold and impersonal, but perhaps that was due to its dilapidated condition. 'I always thought Exmoor was in Somerset, not Devon.'

'Exmoor straddles both counties. Hawks Hall is in a fairly isolated spot just inside the Devon border. It was quite a significant building it its day. The local record office even hold the original construction drawings. It's got an interesting history. Ironic, too, given your circumstances.'

I gave her a sharp look. 'Meaning?'

'It was built in Victorian times as a House of Mercy – a home for unmarried mothers run by a religious order called the Clewer Sisterhood.'

I shivered. 'That sounds scarily like those Catholic

laundries in Ireland which exploited pregnant girls in disgusting conditions.'

'There's nothing to suggest that Hawks Hall was anything like that. The original grounds for setting up the House of Mercy movement was a recognition that there was far too much condemnation of single women who fell pregnant and precious little action to help them, particularly by the Church. While the Victorian period is renowned for being an era of philanthropy and good works, its negative attitude towards so-called fallen women meant provision was woefully inadequate. And what existed was mostly in London and the south-east.'

'And was it a House of Mercy when I was born?'

Esme shook her head. 'Oh, no. The sisters had long gone. They moved on in the fifties, due to costs of upkeep of the building, mainly. And fewer women wanted to join a religious order by then, of course.'

'And then it became a hospital?'

'So it seems, though I'm not exactly sure when or for how long. It was empty for years after the Clewer sisters left, apparently, but dates are all a bit vague after that.'

'But a hospital would keep records, wouldn't they? Couldn't we access those for the time I was born?'

'Yes, except patient records are subject to 100 years' closure rules, on confidentiality grounds.'

'But they're mine,' I said, stiffening.

'And if they existed, you'd be able to make a case

for seeing them. But so far, none have shown up on the archives' catalogue. That doesn't mean they don't exist. Files marked "miscellaneous" can sometimes yield something useful.'

I rested my elbow on the table and dropped my chin on to the heel of my hand. It didn't sound very encouraging. Too many ifs, mights and maybes.

Esme leaned over and dug into her bag. 'What I didn't tell you,' she said, laying some estate agent's particulars on the table, 'is that Hawks Hall is on the market.'

'Really?' I sat up straight and snatched up the stapled pages. The photograph I'd just been looking at was displayed on the front cover.

'And it just so happens,' Esme continued, 'that there's an open day at the weekend. I thought I might take a trip down to Devon and take a look.'

I looked up. 'Can I come?'

Esme grinned. 'Why not? There are bound to be a few locals having a nose around. We might learn something to our advantage.'

7

Esme picked me up early, to avoid getting caught up in Bristol's bottleneck of Saturday shoppers heading for Cribbs Causeway's retail park, she said. The weather held promise, with weak sunshine in touchable distance behind the clouds, but it deteriorated as we drove south. I hoped that wasn't an omen. I asked Esme what she thought my chances were for finding out what I wanted to know but she wouldn't be drawn. One thing leads to another, she told me. It's a matter of joining up the dots. Sometimes slowly.

The North Devon Link road was a tedious long line of traffic and it was a welcome change to turn off towards Exmoor. But soon my stomach began protesting at the twists and turns of the Devon lanes and I was relieved when Esme turned into a stony track and slowed the car to a crawl.

'Where are we?' I said, peering out into the grey February drizzle.

'This is it, apparently. Or pretty close, anyway.'

'You're kidding me.' The mist obscured everything beyond the end of the bonnet. 'But there's nothing here.'

Esme inched along a bit further until the rear boot of a large black Range Rover came into view. She pulled the car to a halt behind it and cut the engine. 'Seems like as good a place as any to park up,' she said, unclipping her seatbelt.

She opened her door and climbed out. I did the same and went round to the boot, where Esme handed me my jacket. Even zipped up its protection was limited. Esme was much better kitted out in a waterproof coat with a hood.

She slammed the boot lid and zapped the car lock. 'Ready?'

'I hope you know where you're going,' I said, as we trudged down the track. I scanned around. 'Can't see any other punters.'

'Can't see anything much, full stop,' Esme laughed, pulling her hood tighter around her face. 'Let's just follow this row of cars.'

I shoved my hands in my pockets and looked across the ditch which ran down the length of the track. The only evidence of the moor I could make out in the low cloud was a narrow green margin of fine grassland, which was peppered with small boulders and tufts of coppery dead bracken. The drizzle swirled around us and I shivered. 'Bleak, isn't it? And isolated.'

'It's less than two miles from the nearest village in that direction,' Esme said, waving her arm westward. 'But I know what you mean. Odd place for a hospital. Oh, here we are.'

Out of the mist, the bodies of two more large stationary vehicles loomed ahead of us, their nearside wheels up on the verge. We hurried past them and turned left alongside a stone wall towards an open field gate where Hawks Hall came into view.

The house looked larger in real life, peering out menacingly from behind trees, as though watching for unwary trespassers. It seemed the least benign location in which to bring a baby into the world.

Through the gate the track became a wide, open space, scruffy and overgrown. Someone had cut back enough undergrowth to create a path to the front entrance. The huge front door was open and a young fresh-faced man with spiked hair stood on the threshold, a clipboard clutched against him. Ahead of us a middle-aged couple stopped to speak to him. As we got closer, I could see others approaching from the other direction. The open day had attracted quite a crowd.

As we reached the entrance, the couple ahead of us moved inside. The agent greeted us with a nod and waved a copy of the property details at us. Esme stopped to talk to him while I slipped inside to look around.

Evidence of a property long abandoned lay everywhere.

Dry leaves littered the floor of the entrance hall and mould grew in dark swathes up the wall. The first room was sparsely furnished with several old-fashioned easy chairs, tufts of horsehair bulging out of faded covers where mice had chewed into the stuffing. Ivy hung outside the window, further obscuring what little light might have penetrated the grubby glass. A huge fireplace dominated the far wall and the hearth was heaped with damp, black debris from the chimney, emitting a strong sooty odour. I retraced my steps and met Esme in the hall.

'Whoever takes this on is going to have to have a pretty healthy bank balance,' she said, looking up the stairs.

I steered her down the hallway to the room at the back. 'Learn anything?'

She shook her head and wrinkled her nose. 'Doesn't sound like he's been briefed much. All he seems to know is that it's been empty for a while.'

I snorted. 'Bit bloody obvious, isn't it?' I looked about the room we'd come into. At one end was a large Formica-topped table with painted benches. At the other was a kitchen and evidence on the walls and ceiling that it had once been two rooms, knocked into one, probably, to create a large eating area. The couple who'd been ahead of us were standing in a corner, huddled over the agent's particulars, murmuring to one another and pointing to items on the sheet. I looked round towards the door as more voices could be heard from the hallway.

'Let's look upstairs,' Esme said, pulling away.

We manoeuvred around the newcomers and made our way down the hall and up the stairs. I counted six bedrooms and an over-sized bathroom, which I guessed had once been a bedroom. A toilet with an old-fashioned high cistern and chain sat in one corner and a roll-topped bath, in need of re-enamelling, stood isolated in the middle of the room. There was a badly stained wash-hand basin beside the door, over which was an ancient hot water instant boiler. 'All the mod cons, then,' I said. 'I can't imagine this was ever a warm room.'

We retreated on to the landing. Downstairs the hum of voices had increased and it was clear that more people had arrived. We moved along, peering inside the rooms as we went. Each held a single divan bed, stripped of its bedding, and a cupboard sitting on the grubby remains of torn linoleum.

'Seen enough?' asked Esme. I nodded and we descended the stairs and turned left at the bottom to the other side of the house. A small room, housing a modest chesterfield covered in a torn throw of indistinguishable colour, probably had the greatest potential for creating a pleasant space. From here a door led out to what the estate agent grandly referred to as the conservatory but which was more like a hastily constructed glazed outhouse added as an afterthought with whatever incongruous building materials had come to hand.

The middle-aged couple were examining its finer points so, with a brief nod of acknowledgment, we passed on through and went outside into the yard.

Esme stood back and looked up at the back wall, pulling the particulars out of her pocket and studying them, and occasionally glancing down at the side of the house.

'What are you looking at?' I asked, peering over her shoulder.

'Just trying to make sense of it. Something doesn't match up.'

'How d'you mean?'

She was stopped from answering by the sound of raised voices from inside. 'What's going on in there?' Esme said, looking at me. I shrugged and we hurried back indoors. The woman we'd passed a moment ago was pinned in the corner of the conservatory by an elderly lady. As we arrived a middle-aged man with a grey beard appeared from the hall, pushed his way past the intrigued viewers and intervened.

'Come on, Mother, you're upsetting the lady,' he said, taking her elbow.

She shook him off. 'Well 'er needs to know, Arthur, if 'er's thinking of buying the place.'

The agent appeared in the doorway and hurried across the room. 'Is everything all right here?' he said, flicking his gaze around anxiously.

'This lady just told me that this used to be a hospital,' said the woman in the corner.

'No, a maternity home, not a hospital,' said the elderly lady. 'Ain't that right, young man?'

'I believe so, madam.'

I shot a look at Esme, who looked back with raised eyebrows.

'It doesn't mention that here,' the woman said to the agent, indicating the notes. 'Only about its early history. Why's that?'

'I'm afraid I can't comment,' the agent told her. 'I didn't write the details myself.'

'So you don't know nothing 'bout the scandal, then,' said the elderly lady.

The agent coloured. 'No, certainly not.'

'Scandal?' I said. 'What sort of scandal?'

The old lady turned towards me, her eyes bright in the centre of her wrinkled face, clearly delighted she'd piqued my interest. 'They closed down soon after, see. It wore the ruin of it, I reckon. Bad publicity, you know.'

'What happened?'

'Poor girl run away, didn't she?'

'That's enough, Mother,' Arthur said, trying again to take her arm. This time she relented. 'This young man won't thank you for spreading malicious gossip. Let's get you home.'

The agent looked visibly relieved. 'Drama over, ladies

and gentlemen,' he said, trying to herd the crowd of onlookers who'd gathered to see what was going on back along the hall. 'Do carry on. There's still plenty of time to look around.'

I wandered after Arthur as he led his mother out of the door and away down the path, keen to know if the old lady had more to say. I felt a jab in my ribs.

'See what you can get out of the agent,' Esme hissed as she pushed past me. 'I think he knows more than he's saying. See you back at the car.'

I watched as Esme caught up with Arthur and, smiling, engaged him in conversation.

As they reached the middle of the yard, the old lady stopped. She turned back to the gathering crowd of viewers who, like me, had ignored the agent's announcement and had followed on outside. 'And I'll tell you this,' she shouted to the enthralled onlookers. 'That poor maid wore terrified.'

8

I pulled myself upright from my slouched position against the bonnet of Esme's car, as she arrived back at the rendezvous. 'Anything?' I said.

'A lot of jumbled thoughts which Arthur insisted were just "tittle-tattle". Nothing more than what she'd already said, really, though with more emphasis. But he did at least confirm it was a private maternity home, and for unmarried teenage girls, it seems. Though no one locally went there, from what I gather.'

'So my biological mother was probably a teenager.' I thought back to my own teenage years and tried to imagine what that would have been like. What were her circumstances and why did she come here?

'So how about you?' Esme said. 'Get anything useful from the agent?'

I shook my head. 'I don't think he knew what she was on about. He seemed to think the stories were all about the place being haunted.'

'Well, if anything significant happened, it might have

been reported in the local press,' Esme said, opening the driver's door. 'Which means a delve into the local newspaper archives. So, unless I turn up anything online, I could be back down here again on Monday for a trip to the record office.'

'If you do,' I said, catching her eye over the car roof, 'can I come with you?'

'Aren't you working?'

'I'm on extended leave. Someone at work said it was best dealing with stuff sooner rather than later.'

Esme raised an eyebrow. 'Bet they didn't realise quite what that meant in your case.'

'No. I'm sure they didn't. Or just how much *stuff* Mum left me to deal with. I can't believe it. She kept, like, everything. It'll take me years to sort it.'

'A valuable family-history resource treasure trove, then?'

'I wish. It all looks pretty boring. House insurance policy booklets, instruction manuals for things she didn't even have any more and electric bills going back, like, forever.' Nothing of any use in establishing the truth of my birth, if that's what Esme meant. 'So?' I said. 'Can I come?'

Esme considered for a moment, then smiled. 'Sure. Happy to have your company.'

9

Monday morning found me sitting in Esme's car in front of the record office while Esme went to buy a parking ticket, hoping my decision to come had been the right one. Should I have stayed home and used my time practically, sorting out the chaos of Mum's house? Or, better still, gone out with friends and get a million miles away from what was feeling like the pressure of the dark clouds of a threatening storm?

I told myself to get a grip and stop ducking the issue. I knew full well I didn't want to hang around waiting for information to be passed on in a phone call. I wanted to be there when Esme uncovered it and I sensed Esme understood that, even though sometimes she looked at me as though she worried whether I might cave in under pressure. But so far she seemed happy enough to have me hanging on her coat-tails. Someone else may not have given me the chance. I'd best not blow it.

A blast of cold air woke me out of my pondering as Esme slapped a ticket on to the dashboard. I got out of the car and we headed across the car park and into the building. 'I hope I haven't got your hopes up,' she said, as we climbed the stairs to the second floor and the archives room.

'But you're pretty confident, right?'

'If whatever happened attracted enough attention, it'll have been reported in the local press. That's our best bet for more information.'

'You didn't find it in the newspaper archives online, though. How can you be sure it got reported?'

'I can't. But the online project is still ongoing. There's some forty million pages to scan and they've only done around fifteen million so far. There are huge gaps. So if there was something written about it but it hasn't been digitized yet, it'll be in here on microfilm.'

An odd sensation of nervousness settled in the pit of my stomach as we passed through the swing doors off the top landing. Whether it was in anticipation of the disappointment of finding nothing or fear at what finding something may bring, I wasn't sure.

*

I studied the weird piece of equipment Esme told me was a microfiche reader while she went to locate the films of the newspapers we needed. It looked like an old-fashioned TV in a box, with a canopy at the top and a device below on which I guessed the film would be wound, its contents somehow projected and magnified on the sloping screen

41

inside. Identical machines were set in a row along the tables next to me. Only the one against the wall was taken. An elderly man was alternatively peering into the box and scribbling down notes on a pad in front of him.

Esme arrived at my side and pulled up a second chair, flicking a switch to illuminate the screen as she sat down and tipped out a reel of film from a plastic case. She deftly threaded the spool, winding the mechanism until I could see print appear in front of us. The old lady at the viewing day had suggested that it was the scandal, as she'd called it, which had forced the maternity home to close so we'd decided to search the year of the closure first.

'Do you reckon it would have made headline news?' I asked Esme.

'That would be easier but there's no way of knowing. Some other big story might have pushed it in to the inside pages. But let's scan through the front pages first. It's a weekly paper, so there's only fifty-two to look at.'

I pulled a face. 'Only?'

Esme grinned. 'Patience, that's what you need in this job. And bloody-mindedness. If it's here, we'll find it.'

By the time we'd checked every front-page headline my head was spinning and the print was dancing in front of my eyes. 'I don't know how you do this every day,' I said, pushing my finger and thumb into my eye sockets. 'It'd do my head in.'

'You get lost in the mission and don't notice, I suppose,'

she said, sitting back in her chair and rubbing a finger along the scar on her cheek. She did that a lot, I noticed. I wondered if it itched but didn't like to ask. Did she ever talk about how it happened, I wondered? Maybe one day, when I knew her better, I might dare to pose the question.

'Well,' she said, sighing and poking a strand of hair back in its fastening at the back of her head, 'either it was longer ago than we think, or it was confined to the inside pages.' She leaned forward and began winding the film back on to its spool.

'Can't you work backwards?' I suggested.

'In theory but I find it easier to start from the beginning again. More logical.' She looked at me over the top of her reading glasses. 'Do you want a break? I'm used to it but you look as though you're struggling.'

I shrugged. 'Didn't sleep great, that's all.'

She took off her glasses. 'Why don't you stretch your legs for a bit while I carry on and pop back later?'

The thought of being outside in the fresh air was compelling but it made me sound like a lightweight. 'What? And not be here at the eureka moment? No way.'

She nodded. 'Be a shame not to share it, I admit,' she said, smiling and replaced her glasses 'OK, let's go for it.'

It was almost an hour later that we struck gold. I saw it first, which sort of vindicated my wobbly moment, I thought. "Villagers' concern for runaway young mum-to-be", was the headline.

'Well spotted!' said Esme as we devoured the story. It was only a short column but confirmed the gist of the old lady's account. A young pregnant woman – no name was given – was discovered wandering through the village without a coat and in some distress by the landlady of the local pub. The landlady told the newspaper that she'd realised where the girl had come from and had contacted the maternity home who'd fetched her back.

'That old lady said she was scared,' I said. 'Do you think that's what's meant by her "being in some distress"?'

'Could be,' Esme said. 'But there's nothing about that in the piece. Perhaps the journalist didn't get to speak to her and went digging around after the event. Which suggests to me that he felt there was more to the story than this report implies.'

'Perhaps there's a follow-up in another issue.'

'True. Worth checking.' Esme reached for the spool winder. 'I'll just wind on to... Whoa... Hang on a minute.'

'What?' I said, frantically scanning the screen for what Esme had seen.

'Hey, this is weird.' She pointed to a name on the screen.

'Harriet Monsell?' I said, with a shrug. 'What about her? Says here she ran the maternity home.'

She took off her glasses and turned to me. 'Harriet Monsell was the woman who was a major player in setting up the Clewer Sisterhood I told you about. The House of Mercy.'

I frowned. 'But they were the nuns in Victorian times, weren't they?'

'Exactly. Harriet Monsell died in 1883. So what do you think?' she said, her eyes wide. 'A bizarre coincidence? Or something more ominous?'

10

Outside the library, I sat on the bench and studied the copy Esme had made of the newspaper report. Meanwhile Esme paced up and down a short distance away, her mobile to her ear, calling her contacts in the hope of tracking down the journalist, Mick Sheldon, who we'd established had written the piece. We were keen to find out if he remembered the incident and whether there was more he could tell us. Something akin to a rock lodged itself in my chest as I waited for the outcome of her enquiries and I realised what store I'd put on her optimism for finding him. But what if she couldn't? Who else could we turn to if this option proved a dead end?

I looked up as I heard a change in Esme's voice as she ended the call and headed my way. 'Success!' she said, her eyes shining. She slumped down on the bench beside me. 'Phew. I was beginning to run out of options but then a friend referred me to a colleague of his and he gave me a phone number.'

'So you got hold of him?'

'Yes. And he's happy to meet.' She turned towards me. 'You up for it?'

I stood up. 'Sure. Lead me to him. Where does he live?'

'No, he's coming to us. We're meeting him at his local. I offered to buy him a pint.' She grinned. 'Always a good ploy to hook a journalist.'

'What did you tell him?'

'Only that I wanted to talk to him about what he'd written. He didn't take much persuading. I wonder if that's significant.' She checked her watch. 'I said we'd see him at 1.30 so we'd better get going.'

*

We drove out of Barnstaple to a large village on the outskirts of town and pulled into a scruffy car park off a side street. I looked around. 'Where's this?' I said. The car park sat anonymously in amongst a row of terraced houses.

'Pub's up the street,' Esme said, climbing out of the car.

We turned on to the pavement and headed up the hill. Above us stood the ubiquitous Devon pub, long and low with a thatched roof. Inside the floor was laid to flagstones, a heavy beamed ceiling above and a long bar opposite the door.

We took our drinks over to a table beside the window. 'Let's hope he's got something useful to tell us,' Esme said, sliding into her seat. I hoped so too, though a part of me was nervous about what it might be. Esme had suggested we might have lunch while we were here but I wasn't sure I'd be able to eat anything. I took a sip of wine and wondered whether I should have stuck to tonic water.

'You OK?' Esme asked.

'Yeah, sure. Bit apprehensive, that's all.'

'Well, you won't have to wait long,' she said, nodding towards the door. 'Reckon that's him now.'

I looked round to see a lean man with collar-length grey hair combed back off his face. He reminded me of an aging rock star but, instead of a bass guitar slung over his shoulder, he carried a faded rucksack, all straps and buckles. He strode across to the bar and ordered a pint. While the barmaid filled his glass, he scanned the pub, acknowledging us with a nod. With only one other table taken by a giggling party of young women, it wasn't hard to work out who we were. Sheldon picked up his pint and came over.

'Thanks for the drink,' he said, putting his pint down on the table.

'You're very welcome,' Esme said and made the introductions.

Sheldon sat down opposite the window. 'So,' he said, dropping his rucksack on to the floor. 'Bloody long time ago, this was. Why the interest now?'

'The place is on the market,' Esme said. 'We went to a viewing on Saturday.'

'Thinking of buying it, are you?'

'Needs a hell of a lot of work. It's been empty for years.' She rested her elbows on the table. 'We we're intrigued at something which cropped up at the viewing. An old lady got quite animated about your story of the girl who ran away from the place, didn't she, Gina?'

I nodded. 'She said she was terrified.'

'Like I said on the phone,' Esme said, 'I understand it was you who wrote about it at the time and wondered what more you knew.'

Sheldon took a long draught of beer and wiped his mouth with the back of his hand. 'You're going to a lot of trouble to find out about some local gossip, aren't you?'

I looked at Esme. Mick Sheldon was clearly far too savvy to buy the story that we were potential property developers.

'And you weren't exactly reluctant to come here and tell us all about it,' said Esme. 'So what's your interest?'

Sheldon scratched his chin and stared at her but said nothing.

Esme cleared her throat. 'Perhaps it would help if I told you I've been engaged to do some family-history research.' She waved a hand towards me. 'Gina's helping me.'

He flicked a glance at me before addressing Esme. 'Yeah?'

Esme scowled. 'And what's that supposed to mean?'

'Not after the story, then?'

'What?' Esme rolled her eyes and shook her head, a wry

49

smile on her face. 'You looked me up.'

'Not worth my salt if I didn't do my research, would it?'

I looked at each of them in turn. 'Will someone tell me what the hell is going on?'

'He thinks I'm a journalist,' Esme said, turning towards me. 'Put two and two together and made the proverbial five. He's worried he's about to lose a scoop, I assume.'

'Tim Quentin not your husband then?' put in Sheldon.

'The late Tim Quentin, you mean. And yes, he was and yes, we worked together. But after he died I changed career. OK?'

'Look, you two,' I said, 'can we skip this and get on with what we're here for?' I stared at Sheldon. 'She's not stringing you a line. She is here to do family-history research. Mine.' I thrust a thumb into my chest. 'I was born at Hawks Hall when it was a maternity home and I want to know more about it.'

'Born there?' Sheldon said, stiffening in his seat. 'Bloody hell.'

If I hadn't been struggling to retain my composure, I would have asked him why he was so surprised. But Esme was ahead of me.

'An interesting reaction?' she said. 'Care to explain why?'

Sheldon shrugged. 'Didn't expect it, that's all. Never thought I'd ever get a second chance.'

'At what?'

'At finding out what the hell was going on. Not once I'd got short shrift from the bitch that ran the place. I wanted to dig a bit deeper but I was a rookie back then. What I wanted counted for sod-all. Editor couldn't be arsed. Mothers and babies not exactly a pet subject of his. But there was something I reckoned was worth checking out about the place. And her.'

'You mean Harriet Monsell?'

'Yeah. Evasive piece of work,' Sheldon said. 'Didn't like my questions, that was obvious.'

'Esme reckons she wasn't kosher,' I said and told about the name's historic association.

He nodded slowly, a serious expression on his face. 'Interesting. Could explain why she was so jumpy.'

'So what happened with this girl?' Esme asked. 'Was she reported missing? Is that what happened?'

'Not that I heard. She was found wandering around the village having run away, apparently. I never saw her myself. I'd gone there to report on some fete or other. This girl had gone AWOL earlier in the day and everyone was still talking about it.'

'The pub's landlady found her, didn't she?' I said.

He nodded and downed another gulp of his beer. 'Took her back to Hawks Hall and that was the end of it.'

'The old lady said she was terrified?' I said. 'Do you know what of?'

'Ranting on about it not being safe up there, according

51

to the landlady. Babies were dying, she said.'

'Dying?' I shivered.

'So she alleged.'

'There's no mention of that in your piece,' Esme said.

Sheldon shook his head. 'Landlady wouldn't be quoted on it. Said the girl was off her head. Reckon she didn't want to get involved.'

'She still there?' Esme asked.

'Nah. Long gone. Reckon she told me all she knew, anyway.'

'So where do we go from here?' I said, addressing Esme. In my peripheral vision I saw Sheldon reach down for his rucksack and pull out a brown envelope. I flicked my head around. 'What have you got there?' I asked, watching as he reached inside the envelope. He pulled out a grainy photograph and laid it on the table.

'Not sure if this is any help but you're welcome to a copy.'

Esme reached across the table and slid the photo towards us. I peered at it eagerly. I recognised the setting at once as being the front facade of Hawks Hall. Half turned away from the camera was a woman. 'Harriet Monsell,' said Sheldon, tapping the image. 'She didn't take too kindly to being photographed. She made a grab for the camera and I had to make a quick getaway.'

I peered at the woman, scowling out at me, a scarf wrapped round her head in bandanna style, a fringe of blonde hair poking out from underneath. As I did so, my eye fell on another figure in the background of the photograph. I swung from elation to dread in a heartbeat, the shock of recognition forcing me to cry out.

'What is it?' Esme said, resting a hand on my arm. 'What have you seen?'

I placed a shaking finger on the image.

'Oh that's Lance Jarrett,' Sheldon said. 'Her toy-boy. Not one of life's grafters, from all accounts. Bets, booze and fast cars – preferably if someone else was paying. He look familiar, then?' he added, picking up his glass.

I swallowed and looked at Esme. 'That's him,' I said, my voice hoarse and unsteady. 'That's the man in Mum's house.'

11

I was hardly aware of the rest of the conversation between Esme and Sheldon. The man's image kept swimming in front of me, the gaunt face, the wild, bloodshot eyes. But perhaps it was all in my imagination. Maybe my subconscious was superimposing the intruder's face in a desperate effort to make a connection. After all, he'd be thirty years older than in the photograph. I could easily be mistaken. Perhaps the idea of a terrified pregnant young woman running away from a traumatic situation was playing strange tricks on my mind. But deep down I knew that wasn't true. Jarrett was in Mum's house and I needed to know why.

My thoughts were interrupted by the scraping of Sheldon's chair on the flagstone floor as he stood up. Esme agreed to keep him informed and, with a nod in my direction, he left.

Esme laid a hand on my arm. 'Do you want to go on with this? I'd quite understand if you decide it's best left alone. Or you can stay out of it, if you like. Let me see what I come up with.'

I shook my head. 'No,' I said, snatching up my glass and drinking it down in one go. 'I want to know what that man...' I banged my glass down as something registered in my head.

'What's the matter?' Esme asked.

'There was the letter J written in Mum's diary.' I turned to her. 'Do you think it stands for Jarrett?'

*

We retreated to the library and found a table upstairs in the reference section where Esme booted up her laptop. On the way, Esme filled me in with what little information Sheldon had to pass on which was that Jarrett had Shropshire connections. No one that Sheldon had spoken to at the time the girl had run away had considered him much more than a hanger-on and that it was Monsell who was the workhorse.

'So what are we looking for?' I said, sitting down next to Esme. It was going to be difficult to concentrate. I wanted to get back to Mum's house and see if I could find any evidence that Jarrett and Mum knew one another.

Esme clicked the mouse and brought up a database search engine on to the screen. 'Ideally, we could do with finding someone else in your situation,' she said, entering information into a series of boxes.

'How can we do that?'

'Your birth was registered locally so I assume so was every other baby born at the home. Mmm...yes, thought that might be too easy.' She swivelled the laptop so I could see the screen. 'Over 1,600 births that year. I can hardly get certificates copies of every one registered in the hope of tracking down someone with the same details as you.'

'What about deaths of babies?' I said, suddenly remembering the young woman's claim that babies were dying at the home. Esme pulled round the laptop and changed the entries.

'Fifteen,' she said. 'Fewer if the birth and death are the same month, suggesting they died at birth or soon after.'

'So couldn't you check that out?'

Esme wrinkled her nose. 'I think I'd like to know a bit more first. We can't be sure how much store to put on that poor girl's story.'

'But what if she was telling the truth? No one believed her then and we're shying away from it now. Perhaps what was going on was something terrible. The place closed soon after. What's to say they were scared of being found out?'

'You're not seriously suggesting it was a place of disposing of unwanted babies?' Esme said, looking at me in horror.

I shrugged. 'I know it sounds a bit far-fetched but you said Harriett Monsell was Victorian. Didn't that sort of thing happen back then – women taking on babies for money and then killing them? What were they called? There was some famous case where a woman was caught throwing babies' bodies into the Thames.'

'You mean baby farmers.'

'Yes, that's it.' I nodded vigorously, certain that I'd stumbled upon something. 'They advertised in newspapers, didn't they, offering to adopt but it was actually a thinly veiled offer of murder?'

'Gina, I hardly think –'

'They did, though, didn't they?'

Esme took off her glasses and looked at me, her expression serious. 'We're talking a different era, though, Gina. In Victorian times illegitimacy was a huge social stigma and there were few options for a pregnant woman. The threat of the workhouse was ever present and you know what terror that instilled in people. But here,' she tapped the screen, 'we're talking twentieth century. Social Services, adoption agencies, state support for the mother to bring up her child – why would anyone need to resort to infanticide?'

It was a fair point. But I still felt we were missing something. 'You don't think that for this woman to take on some sort of Victorian persona it suggests she's also taken on the same modus operandi?'

Esme shook her head. 'No, I don't. And I would point out that the *real* Harriet Monsell's modus operandi was a world away from taking on babies and keeping them dosed up with laudanum until they faded away from neglect. She was a force for good.'

I hugged myself. 'I can't believe those women got away with it.'

'Infant mortality was high back then. A baby dying at a few months old wouldn't be seen as out of the ordinary.'

'Why weren't they just put up for adoption? Proper adoption, I mean.'

'Because, other than within families, it wasn't the norm and wouldn't become so until after the First World War. Orphans were generally brought up in institutions. It had a lot to do with people believing that an illegitimate child would inherit its parents' bad character so no respectable couple would consider it.'

I sat back into my chair and sighed. 'OK, I see what you're saying. But that poor girl was terrified of something. What? And what happened to her after she was taken back to Hawks Hall?'

'Good question. One we should put to the one person we know can answer it.'

'Who?'

Esme snapped the laptop shut. 'Lance Jarrett. At the moment he's our only lead. We need to find him.'

12

It was getting dark by the time I drove back home from Esme's, where I'd left my car. As I pulled to a stop outside my house, I suddenly became aware of my vulnerability. Had Jarrett got what he wanted when he came to Mum's house or did he plan to come back for another look? And more worrying – though I'd not voiced it to Esme – was he out there watching me, wondering what I knew?

I closed my eyes and took a deep breath. This wasn't going to work if I let myself get screwed up like this. And it wasn't as though Esme had suggested *I* search him out. In fact, she was most insistent that should I see him I give him a wide berth. She'd also pressed me again about involving the police. But until I knew the connection between Jarrett and Mum, I intended to keep things to myself.

Meanwhile, Mick Sheldon was still keen to get his story. He and Esme had come to an arrangement. He'd dig around to see what he could come up with and Esme promised to share with him anything she uncovered too.

I grabbed my bag and climbed out, slamming the car

door and casting around to reassure myself that I was alone and that it was only my imagination which was unnerving me. Besides, he didn't know where I lived – did he? No, of course not. It was only Mum's house which interested him.

I pressed the key fob to lock the car, the flashing lights and high-pitched electronic beep echoing around the street seeming more noticeable than usual. As I crossed the pavement to the front door of my terraced house, I tried not to think about tomorrow when I'd be back at Mum's place. 'One thing at a time,' Esme had said to me as we'd parted, when I'd expressed my fears at the seemingly impossible tasks ahead. Then I'd been adamant about finding out the truth. Now, back on my own without Esme's reassuring confidence, I wasn't so sure.

*

The world always looks better in the cold light of day, so they say, and as I pulled back the curtains on a hazy sunny morning, my optimism and determination had returned. Who was Lance Jarrett anyway? Some loser who'd lived off the back of Harriet Monsell, if Sheldon's information was to be believed. He didn't scare me. I peered up and down the street from the bedroom window, willing him to be out there so I could tackle him in my new-found bravado. But no one was looking back at me and no one was loitering in any of the doorways of the houses opposite.

*

An hour later I stepped inside Mum's hallway and kicked the door closed behind me. The silence enveloped me like a cloud and new tears threatened to undermine my positive mood. I made my way to the kitchen, avoiding the front room, knowing that I'd only look out of the window to see if Jarrett was watching. While confirmation that he wasn't would be a comfort, I wasn't ready to deal with him should he be lurking in full view.

I stored the carton of milk I'd brought with me in the fridge, thinking it was uneconomical keeping it switched on just for that but being unwilling to act on the thought. I filled the kettle instead and made myself a coffee. I'd need some sustenance before tackling the job I'd told Esme I'd do: to see if I could find any evidence that Mum knew Lance Jarrett. I'd already gone through her well-thumbed address book when informing all her friends about her death so I knew his name wasn't there. But Esme had smiled and suggested it might be worth looking a bit deeper, just on the off-chance.

I took my coffee into the office. If Lance Jarrett's name didn't appear in Mum's address book, where else was there to look?

A growing pile of correspondence lay on the desk, screaming for my attention. I sat down and sipped my coffee, staring down at the assortment of envelopes. Bank statements, household bills, circulars and other junk mail. Could there be something here? Perhaps there was a letter, something personal amongst the anonymous formality. I set down my mug and began sifting through the pile.

But I found nothing. Not even a belated sympathy card. I slumped back in my chair with a sigh when the phone rang out, its noisy intrusion sending my sensors to high alert. I took a moment to calm myself before snatching up the receiver. 'Hello?'

Silence. I pressed my lips together. I wasn't in the mood for cold callers, particularly ones playing silly games. 'If you've got something to say, then say it,' I said, with an exaggerated sigh. 'Otherwise piss off.'

I went to put the phone down when I heard a voice. I closed my eyes. Oh, brilliant. Now I'd offended someone who'd probably phoned to pass on their condolences. I put the phone back to my ear and opened my mouth to apologise.

'...poking around where you shouldn't,' I heard the caller say.

'What?' I said, confused. 'Who is this?'

'Keep your pretty little nose out of it, love. Or you'll be sorry.'

My skin chilled as I realised who was on the line. I gripped the handset, anger consuming me. 'I know who you are, you bastard,' I yelled.

But the line had already disconnected.

13

I threw down the phone and let out a loud scream, before sweeping my arm across the desk, scattering everything on to the floor in a gesture of frustration and fear.

When I'd regained my composure, I phoned Esme. Her calm response was a comfort.

'We have to assume it was Jarrett.'

'Got to be.'

'Which suggests we've stepped on someone's toes.'

'So what now?' I said. I looked down at the chaos on the floor. 'Apart from clearing up the result of my freaking out,' I said, relieving the tension with a half laugh.

'That's up to you, Gina,' Esme said.

'Meaning you think I should talk to the police?'

'I understand why you're reluctant but threats are another thing altogether.'

I slumped over the desk and rubbed my eyes. 'I hate this. It's not fair. Why should finding out what I should already know by rights be so...' My brain was so frazzled I couldn't think of the right word.

'Perilous?' Esme suggested. 'Painful? Emotional?'

'All those,' I sighed. 'And more.'

'It will always be emotional. But it doesn't need to be perilous.'

I imagined a conversation with the police, the intrusive questions, being cornered into confessing what I'd stumbled across about my birth and shuddered. 'No, I can't. I don't want my private life blasted wide open, thank you.' The line went quiet. 'Esme?'

I heard Esme sigh. 'There may come a time when you have no choice. You understand that, don't you?'

I thought about what she'd said when we'd first met, that we may uncover more than we'd bargained for and to be prepared. 'I realise that. But when I know the truth, it'll be easier, won't it? But if I flag it up now, they'll take over and I'll lose all control.' I waited. Would she refuse to stay involved? Would she even go to the police herself? 'Please, Esme,' I said, when she didn't respond.

Another sigh. 'Well, at the very least, log everything. And if you see anyone outside the house acting suspiciously, don't take a chance. Report it straight away and get some footage on your phone.'

'OK. I get it.'

'Good.' Esme cleared her throat. 'Gina, I think it would be sensible for you to have some time to think about things. Give me a call tomorrow and let me know how you're feeling. Then if you still want to carry on –'

'Carry on? Of course I want to carry on. That bastard is not going to get away with intimidating me. And I'll do as you say. I'll make a log of everything that happens and if he tries anything, I'll report it. I will.' I took a breath. 'I need to know, Esme. I can't escape that, no matter what I do, can I?'

There was a pause down the line as Esme considered. I was about to threaten her with my option of finding someone else if she wouldn't help but bit back the words when it struck me. 'Oh God. I'm so sorry, Esme. This isn't just about me, is it? If I go down this route, I involve you. You have to agree to getting embroiled as well in such a risky situation.' She mumbled something which I didn't catch. 'Sorry? What did you say?' She didn't answer. 'You've gone very quiet, Esme. What are you thinking?'

'Look, let's use Jarrett's phone call to our advantage. We'll let him think he's warned you off and turn our attention back to Harriet Monsell instead.'

'But she's not real,' I protested. 'We'd be wasting our time. You said yourself, it was likely to be a made-up name.'

'And I haven't changed my mind but I've an idea brewing as to where we might find her.'

A shot of adrenalin surged through me. 'Go on.'

'I can't talk right now, I'm afraid. I'm meeting a client.'

I bit my lip. 'Sorry. I'm taking up your time. You've got other things to do.'

'Don't be silly. I'm glad I was here when you called. Let's meet up tomorrow. And we'll make a plan.'

14

I knocked on Esme's door the next day with some optimism. She had sounded positive on the phone and I was keen to hear what she had to say. The door opened and Esme gestured me inside, her phone against her ear.

While I waited for her to finish her call I wandered over to the opposite side of the room and browsed the bookshelves. Unsurprisingly, many of the titles were history-based. *The Annals of London*, *Maps for Historians* and several editions of old photograph collections of the counties of England by someone called Francis Frith. On the desk stood a framed photograph of a dark-haired man in his thirties, wearing a thick high-necked pullover. Tim Quentin, I assumed, Esme's late husband who Mick Sheldon had referred to when we'd met in the pub. I knew Esme was a widow when I was given her name and there'd been some suggestion of a tragedy behind his death, but no details. I turned away, as though I was intruding, and went and sat down on the sofa to wait for Esme to finish her conversation.

From the expression on her face, the call was good news. She kept looking at me and raising her eyebrows. Everything became clear as she said goodbye to the caller.

'OK, thanks, Mick. Keep me in the loop.'

'Mick Sheldon?' I said, as she cut the call.

'Yes.' Her eyes shone. 'He's been asking around the village. See what he could dig up.'

'He's really got a thing about this, hasn't he?'

'This story's been gnawing away at him for years. You could see that when we met him. It happens like that sometimes. Difficult to resist the chance to pick up with it again.'

I nodded. I'd never thought that much of journalists. In my mind they were justifiably denounced for sensationalism and for hounding people at times of trauma. But if their goal was to expose wrongdoing, then maybe I should adjust my point of view. Then again, we didn't know what we were going to find. Maybe I shouldn't let down my guard just yet or I might get my life story splattered across the Sunday papers.

'So what's he got, then?' I asked.

Esme dropped the phone back on the stand. 'To cut a long story short, he thinks he's found someone else in your situation.'

'What?'

'At least,' she held up her hand, 'he's found the parents.'

For a moment I couldn't take it in. 'How?'

'Through the owner of a local B & B. They stayed with her when they came to visit Hawks Hall.'

'Visiting? Sounds a bit tentative to me. How does he know there's a connection?'

'They had a set of baby clothes with them, apparently. But no baby. And, before you ask, no, she wasn't pregnant.'

I imagined my own parents in the same situation. Did they stay somewhere too? Did they collect me like an undelivered parcel? 'Someone's got a long memory.'

'Well, they were friends of friends, apparently. Not complete strangers. Which is why it stuck in her head and how she was able to dig up a name for him. They're called Collins.'

'So has he spoken to them?' I gripped the edge of the sofa. 'What did they say?'

'That's as far as he's got at the moment. He's got an address and is coming up to see them.'

'Up here? They live locally?'

'Yes.' Esme tipped her head to one side. 'Which, of course, reinforces the Shropshire connection with Jarrett and brings me neatly on to my theory of how we might track down Harriet Monsell.'

'Which is?'

Esme jerked her head towards the kitchen. 'Come on through. My notes are in here.'

I followed her into the kitchen and sat down at the table. The washing machine hummed rhythmically in the background, adding a sense of homely comfort to the room.

'Right,' Esme said, dropping down on to a chair opposite me. She pushed up a strand of hair off her face and tucked it into the clip on the back of her head. 'So. We have a Shropshire connection, like I said. At least two sets of parents – the couple Mick has just found and your own Mum and Dad – and Jarrett. For these teenage mothers to end up in a maternity home in Devon, they must have had a reason to choose Hawks Hall. What if someone was promoting the place? What if someone was finding likely candidates?'

'Referring them to Devon, you mean?'

Esme nodded. 'That's exactly what I mean.' She pulled a sheet of paper towards her. 'So, I asked myself, who'd come in contact with pregnant teenagers?'

This was promising. I sat up straight, buoyed by her optimism. 'Social Services. Teenage charities. Drop-in clinics.'

'Quite.' She tapped the paper in front of her. 'I've made a list of the places we might try.' She reached for another sheet of paper and slid it towards me. It was the photograph that Mick Sheldon had taken of Harriet Monsell outside the home. 'We know what she looks like. Someone might recognise her.'

'Great,' I said, staring down at the photo of the woman who held the key to uncovering my true past. 'Where do we start?'

15

By mid-morning I was becoming despondent. Every place on my list so far had drawn a blank. Either it no longer existed, invariably due to loss of funding, or of those still in operation no one recognised the woman in my photograph. I hoped Esme was having more luck.

So I walked into the waiting room of Shropshire Teenage Support's headquarters with dwindling expectation. Four people, three women and a man, were grouped in conference in one corner of the room. None was over thirty. They'd have still been in nappies when Harriet Monsell shut up shop in Devon and disappeared, never mind when she was living life as her former self. But I recalled Esme's comment that success could come from the most unlikely of sources and the importance of not cutting corners.

I pulled out the grainy photograph from my pocket and wandered over. An Asian guy with a scanty beard and a ponytail, holding a clipboard, looked up and smiled at me with an impressive array of white teeth. His colleagues glanced at me and melted away.

'How can I help?' Mr Ponytail said, gesturing to the unit seating on one side of the room.

I declined the offer of a seat and showed him the photo. 'I'm looking for this woman. It's possible she might have worked here some years ago.'

He studied the picture for a moment before shaking his head. 'Not a face I seen round here. Is she lost?'

I smiled at his quaint turn of phrase. 'You could say that.'

'What's her name?'

'I don't know her real name – that's my problem. She's been using an alias.' He gave me a puzzled look and I wondered whether I'd blown it by veiling the situation in suspicion. I dropped my shoulders and assumed a forlorn expression. 'I'm hoping she can help me find my birth mother.'

Empathy replaced puzzlement on his face. 'Right. Get it,' he said, nodding. 'Tough.'

I jerked my head towards the others, one pinning up a flier on the noticeboard and the remaining two with their back to me, deep in conversation. 'Might your colleagues know?'

He held out his hand for the photograph and took it over to each of them in turn. The pair in discussion both shook their heads but, while the one at the noticeboard did the same, she glanced over her shoulder at me and then said something to the guy, who nodded before coming back to me.

'Sorry. No one recognise her,' he said, handing back the picture. 'But Carrie suggested asking Evelyn Lloyd of The Wetherell Trust. She worked here years ago when it was first set up. If anyone knows, might be her.'

'The Wetherell Trust? Where will I find that?'

'You won't. Not this time of day. It's night shelter for homeless people.'

I looked over his shoulder to see Carrie coming over. 'Evelyn works at the library most days,' she said, as she joined us. 'I'd try there, if I were you.'

I stuffed the photo back in my pocket and smiled from one to the other, a sense of anticipation lifting my spirits. 'Thanks for your help, both. You've been great.'

'No problem,' said Ponytail. 'You take care now. And good luck.'

When I got outside I phoned Esme and filled her in. Esme said she knew some of the library staff but didn't recognise the name Evelyn Lloyd. We agreed to meet by the front entrance. I dragged at the screen to end the call and headed across town.

*

I sat on the bench in the square outside the library, under the gaze of Charles Darwin, scanning the faces coming through the archway, watching for Esme. I'd forgotten to ask her where she'd be coming from. I'd just glanced down to check my phone for messages when I felt a tap on my shoulder. I yelped and looked up.

72

'Sorry,' Esme said, pulling a face. 'Didn't mean to startle you.'

'No, it's OK.' Had I thought it was Jarrett? I forced myself to relax. I didn't want Esme to know how jumpy I was. I needed her to think I was up for anything or she'd start talking about going to the police again. 'It's only that I wasn't expecting you from that direction, that's all.'

Esme nodded towards the library beyond. 'I was only a couple of minutes away. Thought I'd nip inside and ask while I was waiting for you.'

'Oh, right. And?'

'Yes, she is working today but she's on her lunch break. Back in...' she checked her watch, '...about ten minutes.'

'Great.'

'Something else good, too. One of the librarians recognised the photo.'

'Brilliant.'

Esme held up her hand. 'Don't get too excited, though. Didn't know her name. Didn't even know why she recognised her. Only that she was familiar.'

'Let's hope this Evelyn Lloyd knows, then,' I said, conscious of a pool of angst seeping into my stomach. Was I setting too much store on this woman having some information for us? It was possible that Esme knew where we might go from here if we hit a wall but I didn't have a clue. I clamped down on the sense of frustration which was threatening to build. There was no point in panicking before we'd even spoken to her.

'Shall we go inside?' Esme said. 'I need to tell you something.'

We found a couple of empty seats huddled around a low table and sat down. I leaned close to Esme and waited expectantly for what she had to say.

Esme flicked a glance around the foyer. 'Mick phoned,' she said.

'He's spoken to those people?'

She shook her head. 'No, not yet. He's been doing some digging into our friend Jarrett's dirty past.'

'Oh?' I felt myself twitch. 'What did he find?'

'A few minor drugs-related convictions. Then there's his more volatile side. He put some guy in intensive care after a fight outside a night-club.'

I grimaced. 'Nice.'

'But the worst was taking a monkey wrench to his employer when he was sacked for turning up to work drunk.'

'God,' I said, wincing. 'Was his boss OK?'

'Only because a couple of the other mechanics intervened and dragged Jarrett off him. Could have been a lot worse. He served time for that.' Esme reached out and squeezed my hand. 'I didn't tell you that to scare you. Only to make sure that you realise who you're dealing with so you'll make that call to the police if you see him again.'

'Sure. I get it.'

Esme looked up and I followed her gaze towards the

reception desk where two women were in conference. 'Looks like we're on,' Esme said, standing up. I looked across as a large lady with a short pageboy hair cut walked towards us – Evelyn Lloyd, I assumed.

I stood up as Esme did the introductions, wondering what Evelyn's colleague had told her, as she looked ill at ease. Esme showed her the photograph. 'She's calling herself Harriet Monsell here,' said Esme, 'but we don't believe it's her real name.'

'And you think she was a work colleague?'

'Not necessarily,' Esme said. 'We think she had contacts here, possibly with the centre. Or another organisation working with young people.'

'The guys at the drop-in centre said you'd worked there years ago and might be the person to ask,' I said, willing her to recognise the woman. But she pursed her lips and slowly shook her head.

'I think I know the face but I certainly wouldn't remember her name.'

A germ of despair stirred in my head. Having no name wasn't going to get us very far. It was looking like a dead end.

'Any idea why it's familiar?' Esme prompted. 'Do you think there's a chance you did work with her?'

'No, I'm sure I'd remembered if we worked together.' Evelyn rubbed her chin and stared at the picture, sighing. 'I just can't think.'

'Perhaps her hair was different?'

I nodded. Good thought. 'Yes. Different colour, different style.'

Evelyn frowned. 'Wait a minute. She wasn't that social worker who got sacked, was she?'

Esme and I exchanged glances. 'What social worker?'

'Hang on a sec,' Evelyn said. 'I'll see if the others can help. May I?' She took the photo and returned to the desk.

'Well, that's the most promising reaction so far,' Esme said.

'But I thought you'd already asked them?'

'The social worker thing might put it into context and jog their memories.' She gave me a hopeful smile. 'Let's hope, eh?'

I gazed over to the desk and watched as Evelyn showed the photo to the librarian on duty. A shake of the head and Evelyn disappeared into an anteroom.

The tension made me restless and I wandered over to the notice board. There were several fliers pinned up about teenager groups not on our list but which might potentially have information for us. But, as I'd discovered, youth groups came and went and we were talking over thirty years ago. What likelihood was there of gleaning anything useful? If we didn't score here, it didn't look hopeful.

Esme called my name and I swivelled round to see

Evelyn on her way back. I hurried over, aware of a tightness in my throat.

'Any luck?' Esme asked, as Evelyn handed back the photograph.

'Bit of a debate.' Evelyn said, gesturing for us to sit down. She dragged over a stool for herself. 'The general consensus,' she said, lowering her voice conspiratorially, 'is that, yes, I was right. She's the social worker who left under a cloud years ago.'

'What sort of cloud?' I said.

Evelyn gave me a wan smile. 'Well, perhaps that's rather an understatement. She was sacked for gross misconduct.'

'God, what did she do?'

'It was all hushed up, of course. Dealt with as internal discipline, even though some said it should have been a criminal case. I suppose they didn't want it to reflect badly on the department. Word was she was caught messing with confidential files.'

'Define "messing with,"' Esme said.

'Well, I'm afraid your guess is as good as mine, though there was talk about her stealing information. But to be honest, everyone has their own personal theory. The only thing we're all in agreement about is that she and the powers that be didn't see eye to eye on policy. But what she actually did...' she threw her hands up in a gesture of futility '...is open to wild speculation.'

'Did you get a name?' I said, unable to hold back any longer.

'Oh yes, I did.' She took the photograph and turned it over. 'I've written it down on the back of your sheet. It's Jarrett. Marilyn Jarrett.'

16

'So what is she? Sister or wife?' I said, peering over Esme's shoulder. She sat at the laptop, checking an online database she called the Marriage Indexes, looking for Jarrett and determine if Marilyn Jarrett – aka Harriet Monsell – and Lance Jarrett were husband and wife.

'Hang on. Nearly there... Yes, here he is.' She pointed to Jarrett's name in a list on the screen. 'Married in 1980 to Marilyn Masters.'

'Well, that's got to be her.'

Esme took off her reading glasses. 'I wonder what she's calling herself these days. Pretty certain not to be Harriet Monsell. She'd want to distance herself from Hawks Hall.'

'Could she be using her real name?'

'That depends, in part, on where she went after Hawks Hall closed. Did she stay in Devon? Move on somewhere else? Or did she return to Shropshire? If she did, with everything that happened with her job, she might have wanted to keep a low profile. I suppose she could have reverted to using her maiden name.' Esme sat back in her chair. 'I could try any and all and see what I come up with, but she's clearly got quite an imagination when it comes to aliases.' She gave me a lopsided grin. 'Perhaps we'd have more luck looking for people with the same names as the movers and shakers of the Clewer Sisterhood.'

'Hey! Now you might be on to something there.'

'Meanwhile, there's another side to this puzzle which we haven't talked about yet.'

'Which is?'

Esme leaned her arm over the back of the office chair and looked at me over her shoulder. 'Having established a contact for their teenage mothers, we now need to work out where they sourced the childless couples, like your parents and the Collinses.'

'OK. And do you have a theory for that too?'

'Not yet. But I might do once Mick Sheldon's spoken to the Collinses.' She snapped her laptop shut. 'Well, we've done all we can for now. Let's wait and see what Mick comes up with.'

*

I gave in to the nagging of friends that it was about time I rejoined the human race and accompanied them on a night out. Whether I benefited from the change of scene was hard to gauge. I felt like I'd stepped into a parallel universe, which, while it was pleasant enough while it lasted, made going back to the real world hang like a heavy cloak on the edge of my periphery, ready to engulf me the moment the evening ended and I said goodbye. I suppose I could have poured my heart out and revealed the agony of my circumstances. But after hugs and sympathy they seem to sense that I wanted to switch off and let my hair down rather than talk. That suited me fine. Keeping the two worlds separate seemed the perfect solution for the moment.

My compassionate leave was fast coming to an end and I'd hardly begun the practical tasks of sorting and clearing Mum's house. I told myself I didn't need to address the wardrobe and drawers of clothes for a little while longer so I spent the next couple of days turning my attention to other cupboards in Mum's house, the impersonal items, such as sheets and towels. Even so, the task brought back enough painful memories of the time soon after Dad died, when Mum seemed to be obsessed with buying things for the house. I remembered getting irritated with her over her irrational behaviour and feeling guilty when she broke down in tears, complaining that I didn't understand the pressure she was under. A friend said it was probably just her way of coping. After that I never mentioned it again. If retail therapy helped her deal with losing Dad, what difference did it make to me? Now, though, I knew the "pressure" she was under manifested itself in much more than Dad's death, which left her to handle matters alone, with no one to turn to for support, least of all, me – the daughter who wasn't her own and whom she was desperate to keep in ignorance. I pushed such sad thoughts to the back of my mind and focused on the job in hand.

I was on the landing emptying the airing cupboard of enough linen to service a hotel, much of it still in its original packaging, when my phone rang and I saw Esme's name come up on the screen. My hand was shaking as I swiped to make the connection.

She apologised for not getting back to me sooner and said she'd phoned to bring me up to speed with Sheldon's visit to Mr and Mrs Collins.

'It's not great news, I'm afraid,' she said. 'They flatly refused to talk to him.'

I sank down on to a heap of bedding. 'So does that mean we're on the wrong track or that they have something to hide?' I wondered what my parents' reaction would be to a journalist turning up on the doorstep asking the sort of questions Sheldon would ask. I guessed it wouldn't be much different.

'They're certainly familiar with Hawks Hall because their son Matthew was born there.'

I sat upright. 'He was? You're sure?'

'Absolutely. I sent for his birth certificate. Hence the delay. I had to wait for it to arrive so I could confirm everything before I phoned you.'

'And was it like mine...?'

'Was Mrs Collins registered as the mother, you mean? Yes. So either she had Matthew at Hawks Hall – which is unlikely, given that the woman at the B & B didn't reckon she was pregnant – or the arrangement was the same. Matthew was adopted.'

'So what can we do?' Frustration gripped me. 'God, Esme. If these people won't tell us anything, how the hell do we make any progress? Because, I take it you've not turned up Harriet Monsell, yet?'

'Nothing so far.'

I stood up. 'Look, what if I go and see them? They might talk to me. Where do they live? Email their address. Or I'll take it now, if you like.' I hurried down the stairs in search of pen and paper.

'Gina, circumstances may explain the Collinses' reluctance. They're going through a bad time at the moment. Perhaps in a few months –'

'A few months?' I stood up. 'I can't wait a few months.'

'I know how you feel,' Esme said. 'And I understand your impatience. But there are two things you should know before you decide to go down that route.'

'What?' I'd arrived in the study. I leaned back against the desk, pressing the phone hard against my ear to stop my hand from shaking. 'What is it I need to know?'

'It seems Matthew died in a car accident four months ago. Tragic for them and a lost opportunity for you, sadly, to share your feelings with someone else in a similar situation to you.'

I felt numb. Another dead end. But it wasn't a dead

end, was it? The Collinses knew something. Correction. They knew everything. I couldn't ignore it. 'I have to speak to them, Esme. I'm sorry for their loss but I have to.'

'I know, I know. I'd feel the same in your shoes. But tread carefully, won't you?'

'Of course. I don't intend to trample over their grief.'

'I'm sure you won't. But that wasn't what I meant.'

'Oh?'

I heard Esme take a breath. 'The second thing you should know. Mick said he thought they seemed frightened.'

17

The Collinses lived on a busy road opposite a playing field. As it was easier to identify the house on foot rather than while driving, I parked in a side street and walked back. I didn't stop directly outside – far too conspicuous. Anyway, I needed to prepare myself. I carried on to the end of the street, pausing at the pedestrian crossing to take stock. A woman holding hands with two children, one either side, waited on the opposite pavement for the traffic to stop and then crossed. I busied myself with my phone until they'd passed and the lights had changed back to green. I was relieved when the woman turned away from the Collinses' house, allowing me to retrace my steps to the street where I'd parked the car.

On the corner I stopped again. Now what? I could hardly repeatedly pace up and down the street without attracting attention. Either I had to go and knock on the door or get back in my car and drive away. I sighed, cursing myself for my indecision. OK, I decided. Go for it.

I took a deep breath and strode boldly towards

Number 43. I had the house in my sights when the front door opened and a man came out – Mr Collins, I assumed. I slowed. Should I approach him or see if someone else was at home?

As Collins emerged on to the pavement, I saw he was accompanied by a black spaniel puppy. They turned right and headed for the crossing. I decided to follow.

As anticipated, Collins turned into the playing field. Around it ran a narrow tarmac park, creating a margin of grass and shrubs at the edge, interspersed with benches. My insides churned around alarmingly and my overwhelming instinct was to turn back and forget the whole idea. But angling a chance at conversation in these circumstances felt considerably more appealing than knocking on his front door so I continued to tag along behind him.

A short way along the path, he stopped and let the dog off its lead where it charged off across the field with unconcealed glee, his ears flapping against his head. Collins whistled and the dog made a wide about turn and bounded back for an affectionate pat from its owner before he game was repeated.

I reached Collins and stopped to watch the dog's antics. 'Clever,' I said, smiling. 'You don't even need to throw anything,'

He looked round at me and laughed. 'Just as well since I damaged my shoulder,' he said, rubbing his upper arm. He was about my height, with thinning grey hair. Flecks of broken blood vessels across his cheeks gave his face a deep red tinge.

'He's obviously loving it. It is a he, is it?'

'That's right. Jasper.'

'How old is he?'

'Coming up nine months, now.' Something about his manner changed, as though he'd been struck by his own words. He cleared his throat and added, 'He was my son's dog.'

I nodded. 'Oh, I see.' I wasn't sure what to say. If I hadn't known about his son's death, would I have made a comment, asked why he was no longer his son's dog? 'Well, he's gorgeous,' I said, deciding to remain non-committal.

We stood in companionable silence while I wrestled with how to make the seemingly impossible leap from dog-talk to the mysterious circumstances of my birth. But, with everything set up for me, I had to try or what was the point of being there?

I cleared my throat. 'It's Mr Collins, isn't it?'

He spun round and gave me a sharp look. 'I'm sorry?'

I held out my hand. 'Gina Vincent.' He took it but I suspect only out of instinct, as his grip was brief.

He peered at me suspiciously. 'Do I know you?'

'We've not met, no.' I waved a hand over my shoulder, in the vague direction of the street beyond. 'Actually, I was on my way to see you when I –'

'See me about what?'

I guessed the approach by Sheldon had made him wary. He must already suspect why I was there. I was crazy to think I would receive any less a reaction. But I had to try.

'I was born at Hawks Hall,' I began.

He turned away. 'I don't know what you're talking about.'

'I understood your son was also born there.'

He whistled for the dog who came bouncing towards him at speed, almost knocking him over. Collins reached down and clipped the dog's lead on to his collar.

'Please,' I said, facing him. 'Will you help me?'

He grabbed hold of the end of the lead and straightened, frowning at me, confused. 'What?' Clearly he was expecting me to say something quite different.

'I never knew before, you see,' I said, aware that this was far from the ordered explanation I'd rehearsed in my head. 'And there's no one else to ask. What do you know about Hawks Hall? What can you tell me which will make sense of what I've found out?'

He eyed me warily. 'And what is it you've found out?'

'That, despite what the records say, it couldn't have been my mother who gave birth to me.'

Collins shot a panicked glance in the direction of the street. 'You didn't speak to my wife, did you?'

I shook my head. 'No. I saw you coming out of your gate with Jasper here.' I bent down and fondled the dog's ears. 'And I followed you. I'm sorry, I don't mean to hassle you. I wouldn't bother you if I wasn't desperate.'

Collins said nothing for a moment. He merely stared while, I assume, he weighed up whether to trust me. 'How do I know you're genuine?' he said. 'You could be just another journalist after a story.'

I dug in my pocket for my purse. 'Here,' I said. I took out my folded birth certificate and handed it to him. 'There, see? Hawks Hall.' I delved back into my purse and pulled out my driving licence. 'And that's me,' I added, 'in case you don't believe me.' I tapped the certificate. 'I'd never seen this before until recently. I had no idea where I was born. Now I need to know.'

'Your parents –'

'Dead.'

He sighed and passed both documents back to me. 'I suppose it hardly matters anymore.' He turned and walked away, leaving me stranded on the path. Did that mean he was willing to talk? He stopped beside a slatted wooden bench and he sat down. I caught him up and joined him. Jasper flopped down on the grass beside us.

'My wife's finding it hard, you see, losing Matthew. Well, it's early days, of course. Though they say you never really get over the loss of a child, don't they?'

'Was he your only one?'

Collins nodded. 'Of course. Too late, by then, wasn't it?'

'Too late?'

'Once we adopted Matthew, we'd shot our bolt for going down the conventional route, hadn't we? They'd ask too many questions about him. Couldn't risk it. Not that it mattered at the time. But if we'd have had others…' He turned towards me, his eyes moist. 'Not that we'd hurt less. I'm not saying that. But, you know. Now she's got no one and there'll be no grandchildren and…' He reached down and patted Jasper's head.

'So Hawks Hall was a sort of unorthodox adoption centre?'

'No questions asked and little information given. Quick and simple.'

'Why not go through the normal channels?'

'Too many hoops. Too long a process. Too much store on looking for the whiter-than-white couple, if you ask me. I was a bit of a daredevil in my younger days. We reckoned that would count against us. Couldn't afford to go down a long route which took years and came to a dead end. We'd wasted enough time as it was.'

'So how did you find out about Hawks Hall?' I asked.

Collins rubbed his chin. 'The wife heard about it. We'd been doing all the fertility stuff and all that.' He slowly shook his head. 'Blind alley. Got nowhere. Hawks Hall was our last hope. A doctor told her about it, I think, but I can't be sure. It was a long time ago.' He stared at me, his eyes narrowed. 'So, now you know. What you plan to do with it, eh? If you send that journalist round again, I'll deny it all. Don't think I won't.'

I gave him what I hoped was a reassuring smile. 'I won't. Promise.'

He put his hands on his knees and got to his feet. 'Well, if that's all.'

I stood up too. 'One last thing.'

He frowned. 'Which is?'

'Did Matthew know? About his adoption, I mean?'

Collins wrapped the lead around his hand. 'I don't see why you'd need to know, but yes. He did.'

'Did he ever try to find his real mother?' Collins said nothing. 'That's what I want to do, you see. But I don't know where to start.'

Collins began moving away down the path. 'I can't help you there.'

'I'm sorry,' I said, tagging along behind him. 'I don't mean to reopen sore wounds. It must have been difficult for you as his adoptive parents –'

'No. You've got us all wrong. We understood why he needed to know.'

'So he did look for her, then?'

Collins stopped, his lips pursed. 'I've answered your questions. Now leave me be.'

'And I'm grateful, I really am. But if Matthew did find his mother, it means he must have got hold of the right information. Did he get it from Lance Jarrett?'

I sensed him stiffen. 'Leave it, love.' He resumed walking.

'He was Harriet Monsell's right-hand-man, wasn't he?'

He snorted and quickened his pace. 'That piece of shite? He's just a nasty piece of work and no mistake.'

'I know. He broke into my mum's house. What does he want, Mr Collins? Do you know?'

Collins stopped and turned towards me. 'Look, love. It's been nice meeting you and all but we're done here, OK? I've already said more than I should.'

I stepped aside and watched him hurry away down the path, replaying our conversation over in my head and trying to work out what was odd about Collins' bitter opinion of Lance Jarrett. Then it struck me. He'd used the present tense. Surely Jarrett belonged to the past, when the Collinses first adopted Matthew?

They'd seemed frightened, Sheldon had told Esme. Was Jarrett the reason? In which case, why was Jarrett involved with them now, after all these years?

I shivered and, with a backward glance around the empty playing field, I hurried away.

18

I walked back to the side street where I'd parked my car, an edginess in my step. Clearly Collins' nervousness had affected me more than I realised. The echo of my footsteps on the pavement seemed unnaturally loud, adding to my sense of isolation, and I found myself glancing over my shoulder regularly to reassure myself that I wasn't being followed. It was a relief to reach the car, climb inside and drive away.

As I pulled into the stream of traffic, I digested everything I'd gleaned from Collins. Although he'd only confirmed what we'd already guessed – that my adoption was far from conventional – his admission that Matthew had attempted to find his biological mother had given me hope that some sort of paper trail existed. I wondered if Esme managed to track down Harriet Monsell yet. Or Marilyn Jarrett, or any other alias the woman had dreamed up. Perhaps I'd call in on her on my way home. Somehow the comforting thought of sharing my encounter with the infinitely sensible and sympathetic Esme Quentin was too comforting a prospect to resist. I took the diversion and headed for her cottage, deciding it was worth taking the risk she'd be at home.

I found her in the front garden pruning a tangled, dead-looking climber against her front wall. A web of knotted grey-brown stems and leaves lay at her feet. She looked round and smiled as I came up the path.

'Hello,' she said, wiping the end of her nose with the back of a gloved hand. 'How did you get on?'

'Not too bad, I suppose.' I nodded towards the stubby twigs in the soil, which was all that was left of the climber. 'Looks like it's had its day. You taking it out?'

'Goodness no. It's a clematis. I'm just giving it its winter prune.' She gestured up the wall of the cottage with a pair of secateurs. 'Come June it'll be a mass of purple flowers right up to the thatch.' She slipped the secateurs into her pocket and pulled off her gloves. 'You'd better come inside and fill me in. I'll update you as well.'

I followed her around the back of the cottage. 'I hope that means you've found the Wicked Witch of the South-West?'

She stopped at the kitchen door to pull off her boots. 'We'll get to that. Tell me about Collins first.'

I sat at the kitchen table and relayed the encounter while Esme washed her hands in the sink.

'He let it slip about Matthew searching for his birth mother and it was obvious he was annoyed with himself. And he nearly freaked out when I mentioned Jarrett.'

94

I told Esme about Collins' comment.

'Yes, I see what you mean. As though he's still part of his life. If you'd not seen him for thirty years, you'd use the past tense, wouldn't you?'

I nodded eagerly. 'Just what I thought. Do you think Jarrett has been harassing Collins?'

'It's possible, given that Collins is so nervous.' She leaned with her back against the kitchen worktop, drying her hands on a towel. 'Obviously we know Hawks Hall is the link between you and Collins but what we still don't know is what Jarrett was after at your mum's house.'

'Is it because he knows I've found out I was born at Hawks Hall and I might blow the lid on it?'

'Why would he assume you have?'

'I don't know but if he *thinks* that, it could be why he threatened me on the phone?'

'I wonder if anyone else in your situation has ever got close to finding out,' Esme said, folding her arms.

'Well, Matthew Collins, obviously.'

'Mmm. I wonder...'

'What?'

She shook her head. 'No, nothing. Well, let's hope he's not watching Collins or he might have seen the two of you together and think you're in cahoots.'

I rubbed my hands down my thighs. It wasn't a comfortable thought. 'So,' I said, determined not to dwell on it. 'How've you got on?'

Esme shook her head. 'Nothing, I'm afraid. No trace under her maiden name, married name or pseudo Victorian philanthropist.'

I pulled a face. 'Oh this is hopeless.'

'I did get a call from Evelyn Lloyd, though.'

I sat up. 'And? Anything?'

'Not in locating her, no. Just some useful snippets of information from the friend she mentioned who'd worked with Marilyn Masters, as she then was. They knew about Jarrett – that he was a nasty piece of work. By all accounts, she took him on as some sort of cause. You know, that she'd save him from himself.'

I scowled. 'Huh. Misguided or what?'

Esme padded across the kitchen and stood by the table. 'I'm sure it won't surprise you to learn that Miss Masters was thought to be a bit of an oddball. Considered herself superior to her colleagues, including her bosses, who she considered lacked vision.'

'Hardly surprising that she fell out with them big-time, then.'

'According to an obituary I read of the real Harriet Monsell, she was admired for striving against public opinion and being committed to a valiant cause.'

'You think Marilyn Jarrett saw herself as someone in the same mould?'

'It's possible. She must have admired her to take on her name.'

'So, is there anything that the real Harriet Monsell did which gives us any useful clues in tracking her down?'

Esme sighed. 'Not that I can see, sadly. It's a shame what Collins told you hasn't given us anything more to go on.'

I leant my elbow on the table. 'Yeah, and I feel a bit stupid about that. If I hadn't mentioned Jarrett I might have persuaded him to say more.'

'Well, you weren't to know that.' Esme rubbed her chin, her expression pensive. 'Interesting what he said about why they'd never adopted another child.'

'Well, they couldn't risk it, could they? The whole reason they'd gone to Hawks Hall in the first place was because he was worried at what the authorities would dig up. Now they were in an even worse place with Matthew's adoption not being kosher.'

'And that, I think,' Esme said, tapping the table with her index finger, 'is where Jarrett comes in?'

I frowned. 'In what way?'

'It's obvious when you think about it. He was in on the scheme.' Esme threw the towel over the back of a chair. 'He knows all their secrets.'

A chill oozed through me as I realised the implication of what she'd said. I blinked. 'He's blackmailing them, isn't he?'

19

Esme disappeared upstairs to change out of her gardening clothes while I lost myself in my thoughts. I wandered over to the kitchen window and looked out into the garden. Early daffodils cast pools of yellow in borders which were otherwise still sleeping. I knew what our conclusion meant. That my parents almost certainly had been black-mail victims too. Could I lay any blame at Jarrett's door for Mum's state of mind, of the stress she always seemed to struggle to contain? While she'd always been a nervous person, she'd got worse since Dad died. She'd have found it ever more difficult carrying the secret alone. And having to deal with the odious Jarrett. My nails dug into my palms as I clenched my fists. How dare he put Mum under so much pressure that she broke? Who the hell did he think he was?

Somewhere, a long way away, I heard Esme's voice.

'Sorry?' I said, dragging my consciousness back to Esme's kitchen.

'You OK, Gina?' She said, a worried frown on her face.

I told her my thoughts and she nodded. 'There could be a good many more people in the same situation.'

'Do you think,' I said, as something occurred to me, 'that Jarrett was at Mum's looking for any evidence which linked him?'

'To get rid of it, you mean?' Esme shrugged. 'It's a logical assumption but surely he'd not stupid enough to allow anything to show up on paper. He'd deal in cash. Worth you having a look, though.'

'Yes, I will.'

Esme sat down and clasped her hands together on the table. 'Gina,' she said, giving me a serious look. 'You may have reached the point where you can't ignore involving the police any longer, you know.'

I pressed my lips together. 'But I might never find out what I want to know.'

'Gina –'

'Think about it,' I said, agitation building inside me. 'If we're right, it means he has all the information I need. I'm sure that's where Matthew got his. Collins knows that but, with Jarrett still on his back, he couldn't afford to confirm it.'

'I'm not sure I like where you're going with this, Gina,' Esme said, colour leaching from her face.

'I have no choice, Esme. It's a no brainer.'

'You're not saying…?'

'Yes, I am. I have to speak to Jarrett first, before we go

to the police. We know where he lives from what Sheldon –'

'Gina, no. You know what his history is, for God's sake. This could get nasty.'

I threw my arms out in a gesture of desperation. 'But once the police get involved I won't get a look in.'

'Of course you will, eventually.'

'Exactly. Eventually. Which could be months, years. I can't do *eventually*, Esme. I need to do *now*. Even if I fail, I have to try.'

Esme shook her head. 'No. You're not going...'

'You can't stop me.'

'...on your own.'

'What?'

'If you insist on going...' she took a deep breath '...then I'm coming with you.'

20

I thought Esme might withhold Jarret's address but she didn't. I told her she didn't need to come, that I wouldn't think any less of her if she changed her mind. But she threw me a scowl of disgust and asked me what sort of person I thought she was. It's the only time I saw her close to angry. I backed off and apologised.

Jarrett lived in a street dominated by a rundown shopping centre of concrete construction and little architectural ambition. We parked in a small car park at one end and walked along the shop fronts, scanning for numbers as we went.

'Why are shops so bad at displaying their street numbers?' Esme complained as we struggled to find any in the first section. 'I'll just nip in here and ask someone.' She peeled off into a hairdressing salon, leaving me on the pavement. I stepped back from the frontages and looked up at the first floor level. A few windows had signs that they were used as storage, with boxes stacked against the windows. Others were hung with net curtains, many grubby and torn.

Now we'd come, I was beginning to think I'd been a bit rash. Telling myself there was no gain without pain did nothing to alleviate my apprehension. But which was worse – going ahead with my reckless plan or owning up to Esme that I'd lost my bottle? No contest.

Back at the hairdresser's, I could see Esme through the plate glass window talking to the girl on reception, showing her the address written on a scrap of paper. The girl was gesturing down the street. Esme nodded and came outside.

'It's that ugly monstrosity at the end, there,' she said. 'Accessed from an alleyway off the main thoroughfare.'

We wandered along, dodging between shoppers. 'Have you worked out what you're going to say yet?' she said, stepping to one side to avoid a boy on a skateboard.

'Not exactly,' I admitted.

'Well, then smile sweetly and leave it to me. I'll talk family-history research to start with. Then we'll see how he reacts.'

Doubts flooded into my mind. 'This isn't going to work, is it?' I said. 'I mean, he's not going to even admit to being involved, let alone pass us any information.'

Esme stopped mid-stride, leaving me stranded two steps ahead of her.

'What?' I said, retreating. 'What did I say?'

'If you're having second thoughts, we can forget the whole thing. Gather up everything we've got so far and take it to the police. Let them deal with Jarrett.'

'But what about Collins?' I said, imagining his anxious face. 'He said if I sent Mick Sheldon round he'd deny it. He'd only say the same to the police. And then the police might think I was making the whole thing up.'

'I'm sure you'd be able to convince them. Your birth certificate and your mum's medical history tells a story in itself. It's where we started, after all.'

I stood, fixed to the spot with indecision.

Esme turned back towards the way we came. 'Come on. Let's go back and think this through properly.'

'No!' I grabbed her arm. 'No,' I said, more calmly. 'I'm just preparing myself for another dead end, that's all. If we don't try, we won't know. And I'd always wonder.'

Esme cocked her head. 'You're absolutely sure?'

I nodded and began walking purposefully towards our destination.

We found the alleyway and ventured down. It came out into a car park at the back. I stood and scanned about. 'There,' Esme said, pointing. The concrete wall running down the alley gave way to an entrance into a stairwell.

We went through the double-glazed doors and began climbing the concrete stairs. Graffiti covered the walls and the stench of urine was overwhelming. 'Bit of a comedown for someone who lived a life of fast cars and luxury,' Esme said.

'Perhaps his little scheme isn't as lucrative as we imagine,' I said.

'Or,' Esme said, stopping to peer at a discarded syringe on the floor, 'his expenses are high.'

We reached the top of the stairs and came out on to a landing which stretched the length of the block.

Esme went ahead, straining to read the numbers on the doors, which were set at regular intervals along the walkway. 'Number 8 should be towards the end,' she said as we made our way along.

Shouts echoed from Number 4 and I flinched as the door burst open. We stood back as two boys rushed out into the passageway, giggling, and ran back the way we'd come. A woman appeared in the doorway, screaming after them to come back. They took no notice. When they disappeared out of sight, she cursed and glared at us. 'What you looking at?' she yelled before going back inside and slamming the door.

'And a lovely day to you too,' Esme said as we hurried past.

'There, that must be it.' Esme pointed to the last flat on the landing. We walked to the end of the landing and stopped outside. The door stood ajar.

Esme looked at me and raised her eyebrows, before rapping the door with her knuckles. 'Hello?' she called. 'Anyone at home?' The door swung open.

We stepped into the dimly lit hall, my eyes taking a few moments to adjust. Esme called again and carried on down the hall ahead of me. I paused to push open the kitchen door on my right hand side when I heard Esme gasp.

'What?' I said, running down the hall. She stood aside so I could see into the living room.

The curtains were drawn, bathing the room in a gloomy orange light. Every cushion was upturned, every shelf emptied, every drawer pulled out, its contents tipped out and strewn across the carpet.

'Someone was desperate to find something,' Esme said, surveying the chaos.

'Yes, but who? And what?' The question echoed with our discussion of Jarrett and his reason for searching Mum's office.

We both spun round at the sound of footsteps in the hall. I found myself looking into a face I recognised. Lance Jarrett.

21

I held Jarrett's gaze for barely a second before he backed off, turned and fled.

'I think we spooked him,' Esme said. 'What d'you make of that?'

But I was already out of the door and after Jarrett.

I figured I had the advantage. I was younger and fitter. And this time I was ready for him. I sped along the landing towards the stairs, hoping my high heels wouldn't wreck my chances of catching him. As I approached the corner I hesitated. Was he waiting to ambush me? But I figured he was more interested in getting away than confronting me so I pressed on.

I hared down the stairs, pausing at the bottom. Which way? Across the car park? No. I could see him away to my left, heading towards the main street, pushing people out of the way as he ran.

I sprinted after him, almost colliding with a teenage girl, who was walking head down, engrossed in her phone. I skirted round her and jogged past until I arrived in the pedestrian square, set back from the road. I stopped to look around, giving me time to catch my breath. Where did he go?

I realised my behaviour was attracting attention. Shoppers were watching me and following my gaze, trying to work out what was happening. I thought I heard someone call my name but as I went to look round, I saw him. He was standing between two parked cars on the edge of the street, looking both ways, ready to cross. Here was my chance. I darted across the pavement and slipped between the back of a black Skoda and the front of a white van. If I was quick, I could intercept him before he moved out.

I was so fixated on Jarrett, I didn't hear the revving engine as the car sped towards me from behind. I felt a jolt as someone grabbed hold of my arm and hauled me backwards. I stumbled, swearing as I fell awkwardly on to the pavement. I heard a thump, the squeal of brakes and someone screamed.

'Are you OK?' Esme said, standing over me. 'I'm sorry but I thought you were going to run out in front of that car.'

I staggered to my feet. My hip hurt and I'd twisted my ankle. 'I almost caught up with him,' I said, rubbing my side and straining to see over the heads of the onlookers gathering on the pavement. Another gaggle of people were huddled in the middle of the road.

'Maniac,' said a woman in front of us with a wheeled shopping bag.

'And he didn't stop, neither,' said another shopper beside her. She clicked her tongue. 'People these days,' she added, shaking her head.

I looked round at Esme. Her face was drained of colour. 'What's going on?' I said, though I'd already guessed.

She steered me away from the bystanders. 'It's Jarrett,' she said. 'That car ploughed into him.' She lowered her voice. 'And, from where I was standing, it looked deliberate.'

22

We drove back to Esme's in quiet contemplation. Police and ambulance had been quickly on the scene and, from the mutterings amongst the crowd, it was clear that the consensus was the same as Esme's. The car driver had accelerated at Jarrett as he'd gone to cross the road. The police had enough witnesses, Esme reassured me. We had no need to stay around.

'Who was it, d'you think?' I said, after a while. I didn't seem to be able to dislodge the harrowing sound of the impact from my consciousness. 'The same person who ransacked his flat?'

'The two events might be totally unconnected.'

'I wonder what they were looking for. The same as us, d'you think?' My brain churned around exploring different theories.

How could I make contact with them? We could help one another.

'We don't know whether either have anything to do with Hawks Hall.'

I shot my head round. 'You can't be saying it's just a coincidence?'

'I'm just saying that, knowing Jarrett's history, it could be anything. We can't jump to conclusions.'

I turned away and stared out of the window, the busy traffic suddenly feeling oppressive in my head. 'I was responsible,' I said, as the horrific truth struck me. 'If I'd not been chasing him –'

'He ran as soon as he saw us, Gina. He'd have still run whether you'd been following him or not. Like I said, you have no reason to assume his bolting had anything to do with why we were there.'

I bit my lip and said nothing more. It was a strange emotion. I wasn't sure how to process it.

*

The accident made the local television news. A fifty-five-year-old man had been pronounced dead at the scene, it reported. It didn't give his name. The police wouldn't release it until his family had been informed. I assumed that included his wife, Marilyn – if, indeed, she was still his wife. The flat had hardly oozed the atmosphere of a happily married couple, even allowing for the chaos they'd found. The thought gave me a brief surge of hope. Where we'd failed, the police might succeed and flush her out. How we'd benefit from their success without inside information wasn't clear but I felt sure it would improve our chances of finding her.

The press had the incident down as a joyrider high on drugs. No one had so far come forward with a registration number and, with the make and model being a silver Ford Fiesta, the police were faced with a huge pool in which to fish for answers. It was hoped that a trawl through footage from the CCTV cameras in the area would identify the car and driver responsible.

I clicked off the TV and threw down the remote. I took some comfort from Esme's words that Jarrett would have run whether I'd pursued him or not, even though I still felt queasy about the manner of his death, especially being so close to the scene. Now, those initial emotions were being overtaken by a sense of loss and frustration, as I faced the consequences of what we'd witnessed. Whatever Jarrett knew about Hawks Hall had died with him. And, despite what Esme said, it seemed likely to me that any documentary evidence that had existed had been removed from his flat. But who'd taken it? Would they use it for their own ends? Or would Collins now be free?

Collins. He wouldn't know Jarrett was dead. Perhaps if he did, he might now be willing to help. I checked my watch. If I left in the next half hour, and assuming Collins walked the dog the same time each afternoon, there was a chance I might bump into him in the park.

As I snatched up my car keys, my phone rang. It was Esme. I told her my plan. 'If nothing else I'll have some good news for him,' I said. 'Heaven knows, he needs some.'

'Gina –'

'Oh, sorry,' I said, laughing. 'I'm chattering on. You phoned me, didn't you?'

'Yes, I did. Look – I've had a thought. It might make you change your mind about seeing Collins again.'

'Oh?'

'Did he say anything about how Matthew died?'

'No, nothing,' I said, puzzled. 'You told me. You said he was killed in a car accident.' Something about her tone bothered me. 'Why d'you ask?'

I heard the rattle of paper down the line. 'I found a newspaper report of the crash. It was a brake failure.'

'God, that's horrible. I had that happen once. It's bloody scary, I can tell you. That's the trouble with driving old cars.'

'Except Matthew's car was less than two years old.'

I swallowed, a knot of anxiety growing in my gut. 'You're saying it wasn't an accident? That someone tampered with his car?'

'If you find out that Matthew *was* searching for his mother and he *did* get the information from Jarrett...shall we say, unconventionally –'

'You mean he stole it?'

'If, Gina. That's all I'm saying. If.'

'And Jarrett found out... Shit!' I recalled something Sheldon had turned up what seemed like forever ago. 'When Jarrett attacked his boss. He was working as a car mechanic.'

112

'Yes. A coincidence, perhaps but –'

'Surely not another one, Esme.' I ran my hand through my hair and dropped down on to the sofa. 'You think Collins knows? But then how could he? The police presumably haven't put two and two together?'

'Even if it had looked suspicious, there would be no way of making a connection with Jarrett. But Collins might.'

I realised what was worrying her. 'You think…?'

'It could have been him in the car that ran Jarrett down.'

23

I sat on a bench beside the playing fields opposite Collins' house watching a group of schoolkids playing football. I suppose I could have knocked on Collins' door and told him that Jarrett was no longer in a position to exhort money but I didn't know how much Mrs Collins knew. But if my hunch didn't work and Collins' dog-walking wasn't determined by the clock, I might yet have to, despite Esme's caution.

'If he was involved in Jarrett's death,' I reasoned, 'he's hardly likely to admit it to me, is he? So as long as I don't accuse him…' Whether she accepted my rationale or not, I wasn't sure but in the end, perhaps because she could see I was determined to go ahead, she sighed and wished me luck. 'Phone me as soon as you've seen him,' was her final instruction.

The whistle blew for full time on the pitch and the players gathered round their coach. Something appeared in my peripheral vision and I turned to see a familiar pair come trotting along the path towards me. Today Jasper was on the lead so he didn't interfere with the players on the field. He was straining against Collins, clearly desperate to join them.

As they came within earshot, I said, 'I bet he'd love to get out there.'

Collins looked across at me and faltered. He turned on his heel and pulled Jasper back down the path. I stood up and hurried after him.

'Leave me alone,' Collins said, staring ahead, avoiding eye contact. 'I've said all I'm going to.'

'Jarrett's dead.'

He registered what I'd said. I could see by his face. But he kept walking. Was this proof that he already knew? That he was the driver? 'It was on the news,' I persisted, scurrying along beside him. 'He was killed in a hit-and-run. You must have seen it.'

He halted and turned towards me, his eyes narrowed. 'How do you know it was him?' His tone was scathing. Spittle formed in the corner of his lip. 'They haven't released a name yet.'

'Because I was there. I was trying to talk to him.'

'That low life? Why the hell would you want to do that?'

'You know why. For the same reason Matthew wanted to. To get the information he needed to find his birth mother.' It was a gamble but it paid off. 'He did, didn't he? He got information from Jarrett.'

Collins closed his eyes and sighed. 'I don't know where he got his information from.'

My insides were jelly. 'But he did find her?'

He shook his head. 'No. He never did.'

I felt my throat tighten. 'Are you absolutely sure? He might have not said. He might have thought –'

'Haven't we suffered enough?' He said, glaring at me. 'This is going to come crashing down on us, isn't it? You've stirred it all up, now. All these years of keeping it…' He tugged at Jasper's lead. 'Come on, boy. Let's go home.'

I watched as he walked back down the path and out of the park before returning to my bench.

It was true, of course. Whatever we'd discovered about Jarrett, about his multi-named wife, about Hawks Hall, would eventually spill out into the known world. I recalled Esme's words on the first day we'd met about not always liking what might be found. But I'd wanted to know. I'd said it would be worth it to find the truth. What I hadn't understood was the impact my revelation would have on others.

Yet that was the irony. I wasn't going to find the truth. If Jarrett had the evidence I needed, it was likely destroyed now by whoever was implicated by it, which, despite Esme's idea that it could be nothing to do with Hawks Hall, I was convinced was Jarrett's wife. She'd not make the same mistake twice. She'd make sure of it.

I blinked away the tears that were threatening to

overwhelm me and called Esme. 'I don't think he killed Jarrett,' I said.

'No, I'm sure he didn't,' she said. 'They've just announced on the local news that a witness has said that the driver was a woman.'

I gripped the phone. 'Jarrett's wife?'

'That's a big leap, Gina. We don't know if she's involved any more or even if she and Jarrett are still in contact.'

I cut the call and sat staring across the grass. The light was fading. I really ought to move and get back home. There was still a chance, I thought, with forced optimism, there was something amongst Mum's belongings to answer my questions. Perhaps, given that she'd been such a hoarder, that there was some clue yet to discover.

I stood up and turned to go, when coming towards me, I saw Collins. He was on his own. There was no Jasper. He walked fast with his head down and when he reached me, he was almost breathless.

'Here,' he said, thrusting a large brown envelope into my hands. 'I don't know if it'll be of any use but you might as well have it.'

'What is it?' I said, taking it from him.

'You were right, of course. Matthew did find his mother. At least he found out who she was but he never met her. He died before he tracked her down. Perhaps his notes may help you.' He regarded me with watery eyes

117

and a determined stare. 'Now go. And, please, for all our sakes, I don't wish to see you again.'

He turned and strode away.

24

I watched Esme as she studied the papers Collins had given me. One sheet showed Collins's name, his address and a reference number. The second showed the same reference number next to the name, Cindy Walker, and a date – Matthew's birth mother, I guessed, and the day he was born.

'Looks like some of these were taken by a mobile phone camera,' Esme said.

I nodded. 'I thought the same. And of some sort of ledger. Was this what he got from Jarrett, d'you think?'

'This is the sort of information Jarrett would need for his little blackmail scheme.'

'So you think we were right? He broke into Jarrett's place?'

She looked at me over the top of her glasses. 'I can't see Jarrett giving it to him voluntarily, can you?'

I took the sheets from Esme and stared down at the images. Somewhere a page existed for me, showing a reference number with my date of birth. And the name of my mother.

'At least I don't have to caution you against house-breaking as a new career,' Esme said. 'We know those files aren't at Jarrett's flat anymore.'

'So we've hit a dead end again.'

Esme took off her glasses. 'Strictly speaking,' she said, her face serious, 'we ought to be hot-footing it to the police to tell them what we know about Jarrett.'

'But we won't, will we?' I said, adding, alarmed. '*You* won't, will you? I can't. Not yet. Not until we've exhausted everything else.'

Esme rubbed a hand across her face. 'I know how you feel, Gina but there comes a point –'

'OK, OK, I get the message,' I said, dropping down on the sofa. 'One last push, eh? What about Matthew's mother? Could we talk to her?'

Esme rubbed her finger along her scar. 'Collins is sure Matthew never got in touch with her?'

'Positive. He was killed before he got that far.'

Esme picked up the envelope and peered inside. 'There's certainly no address here.'

'But we could find her, couldn't we? I mean, I don't know how but you do.'

I sat on the edge of my seat, watching Esme as she mulled things over. But I'd already decided. If she wasn't prepared to take this next step, I was going it alone. It couldn't be too hard, could it?

'OK,' Esme said, standing up. 'Give me a couple

of days and I'll see what I can do.'

'Great. Thanks, Esme.'

'Don't raise your hopes, though,' she said, her expression serious. 'She may be married with a family. Even if I find her, she might not want to rake over the past. I can't force her to talk to us.'

'You will explain about my situation, though, won't you?' I tried to keep my voice steady but my emotions weren't close from the surface. The thought that someone had information and wouldn't share it was almost too much to consider.

'I'll do my very best,' she said.

I nodded. I had to trust her.

25

While Esme did what she needed to do, I forced myself to address my own pressing task – Mum's house and what I was going to do with it. Selling it seemed the only option. It was way too big for me. But I could hardly put it on the market in the state it was. I had to face up to clearing it. And not just the easy impersonal stuff, like those unused towels and sheets, and out-of-date packets of food in the kitchen cupboards. I had to tackle the difficult places – Mum's clothes, private letters, personal mementos and family photographs. But before that I had to confront a place I'd not been able to face since Jarrett's threatening phone call: the office. And, now that we knew about Jarrett's blackmail scheme, I may as well search for any evidence that he'd targeted my parents.

Mum's filing system, despite being all-embracing, was, at least, orderly and I found the last few years' bank statements for the current account easily. Browsing through, I noted regular cash weekly withdrawals of £200. On its own it may, for some people's lifestyle, have seemed insignificant but, knowing my mum, I couldn't imagine her needing such an amount on a weekly basis. But how could I prove it, especially given some of the surplus household items she'd bought in recent years, as I'd discovered from my rummaging in the airing cupboard?

I sighed and pulled open the drawer to put the statements back where I found them, wondering where to look next. As I went to slip the paperwork back, two of the suspension files parted and something underneath caught my eye. I pulled the files apart to reveal a small white envelope lying on the bottom of the drawer.

I pulled it out. It was sealed and across the front in Mum's handwriting was the word *February*. Nothing else. No name and no address. I tore it open. Inside was a bundle of £20 notes. I took them over to the desk and counted them. £800.

I rummaged around on the desk and found Mum's diary. I opened it on the page where the last letter J had been written, the date a week after she'd died. Flicking back through the previous months, I confirmed what I'd noticed before, that the J appeared regularly and checking now, I saw it was always towards the end of a month. Was this the date when the money was handed over to Jarrett? So what of the weekly withdrawals?

Banks usually had a daily limit of the withdrawal of cash from an ATM. So to accumulate such a sum by the appointed date, it looked as though she'd taken out something each week. I picked up the envelope and studied it. February. The appointment she'd not been able to keep. It seemed pretty obvious that this was what Jarrett had been looking for when Mum failed to turn up and hand it over in person. Such an event could only become more common as Jarrett's blackmail victims would, one by one, get older and die, slowly shrinking Jarrett's once lucrative income. It perhaps explained why he'd taken such a risk to break in and get his dues.

I sat back, a little numb and not sure what to do or what to think. If it had ever come to court I suppose my findings would have been dismissed by Jarrett's lawyer as circumstantial evidence. Well, with Jarrett dead, it was irrelevant but it was enough for me.

I tossed the envelope on to the desk as my phone rang.

'It's me,' Esme said, a breathlessness in her voice. 'I've found Matthew's mother. And she's willing to talk.'

26

Cindy Walker toyed with her cappuccino, poking a spoon into the creative pattern in the froth on the top. A nerve twitched in the side of her gaunt cheek, exposed by her unnaturally black hair pulled back over-tightly off her face into a ponytail.

The supermarket cafe was quiet and we'd taken a table in the corner to be out of earshot of the counter staff. I looked to Esme to initiate the conversation. She'd told me she didn't plan to mention Matthew at this stage but be guided by what Cindy chose to disclose. As to her explanation as to how she'd come across Cindy's name, she'd cited the discovery of records from Hawks Hall.

'Gina and I appreciate you meeting us,' said Esme, glancing my way. 'It's been so difficult finding the right people who know enough to help.'

Cindy risked a wary look at me. 'Don't see anything that I know is gonna be any use. Not for finding your mom, anyway. They didn't hold with us getting too pally.'

'What do you remember about Harriet Monsell?' Esme said.

Cindy snorted. 'Matron, she called herself. Liked to think of herself as Mother Earth. Mother Superior, more like, what with all her holy crap about obedience and stuff.' It sounded as though Esme's theory that Marilyn Jarrett modelled herself on Harriet Monsell was right. 'But she was a steely cow,' Cindy continued. 'Not your nurturing sort, that's for sure.'

'Did she mistreat you in any way?' Esme asked.

Cindy shook her head. 'She didn't hit us, if that's what you mean. Locking us up without our dinner was more her style.' She sneered. 'She was a cold bitch, that one. When she wasn't putting on her big act, anyway. She could turn it on like a tap if she had to.'

'So how was it you came to Hawks Hall?'

Cindy shrugged. 'Found myself pregnant at fourteen. Mom doing her nut. Not that she could talk. Had me only at year older and never stopped since.'

'So you have brothers and sisters?' I asked.

'Three of each. Not that we keep in touch. All of 'em 'cept me little sister grew up in care.'

'And your mother?' Esme said.

'Dead.' She looked down at her untouched coffee. 'Overdose.'

'What about your father?'

Cindy looked up at Esme with a smirk. 'What do you think?'

'I assume he wasn't around at this time?'

'Bastard buggered off years ago.'

'So,' Esme said, after taking a sip of her latte, 'you fall pregnant and you're sent to Hawks Hall. I'm interested in who made that decision.'

'Not sure, to be honest with you. Social worker, maybe? I didn't care at first. Thought it might be good, you know, getting out of the way. Place was a madhouse. Never got a minute's peace. I was up for it. That was till I got there. Like bloody boot camp, it was. Work, work, work. No time for telly or playing CDs or nothing. And, like I said, they didn't like it when you got friendly. Reckon that's why they kept you busy. We were well knackered by the end of the day.' She looked away and gazed out the window. From where I was sitting, I could see the glistening of tears in her eyes.

'I'm sorry, Cindy,' Esme said, reaching out and gently touching the woman's hand. 'This must be bringing back some painful memories.'

Cindy sniffed and wiped her nose with the back of her hand. 'Hadn't thought about it in years. Try not to, if I'm honest.'

'There was a report of a girl running away once,' Esme said. 'Do you know anything about that?'

It was clear from Cindy's face that she didn't. 'Did she get away?'

'Picked up in the village and taken back to the Hall.'

'Poor sod. Good for her, though. Wish I'd have had the balls.'

'Do you remember Lance Jarrett?' Esme asked.

Cindy's face puckered. 'Who's he when he's at home?'

'I'm not absolutely sure what his role was but he was Harriet Monsell's husband, though, obviously she didn't call herself Jarrett.'

'Oh, her bloke, you mean. Yeah. Creepy he was. Don't think I ever knew his name. Did sod-all, I can tell you that for nothing. Always hovering in the background. We didn't trust him. One girl said he'd touched her up. I kept a knife under my pillow after I heard that but he never tried it on with me.'

'What happened when it was time to have your baby?' Esme looked at me. 'Gina's birth certificate says she was born at the Hall itself. I assume that was the same for everyone.'

'There was a…you know, where you actually have the baby.'

'Delivery room?'

'Yeah, that's it. The delivery room.' Cindy shivered. 'In the cellar, it was.'

'The cellar?' I said.

Cindy's head shot up. 'What?'

I shook my head. 'Nothing. Sorry.' I glanced at Esme. There'd been no mention of a cellar when we'd visited Hawks Hall.

Esme gave Cindy a reassuring smile. 'Go on. The delivery room was in the cellar.'

'Yeah. We never went down there, normally. Well, not unless you'd broken the rules, of course. But she was always down there, Monsell was. There was a way in from outside, I heard, so she could sneak in and out without anyone knowing, though I never saw it. It was her HQ, like. She ran the place from down there.' A fleeting smile passed across her face. 'We used to call it her lair.'

'And was there a nursery too?' Esme asked. 'A place where the girls brought their babies?'

Cindy looked down at her now cold cappuccino. 'Nah, nothing like that. Never saw the babies. It was always the same. She'd start her pains. You'd hear her yelling and you'd think, that's it now.' She looked up at us, her face drained. 'Once you'd had it, see, they shipped you back home.'

'So you never saw the other girls again?'

Cindy shook her head. 'That's what I meant when I said I didn't see how I could help. Never knew who had a boy, who had a girl.'

Silence fell between us, punctured only by the hiss of the coffee machine at the counter behind and the chattering of the servers.

'And you, Cindy?' I asked, even though I knew the answer. 'What did you have? Boy or girl?'

Cindy's voice was barely audible. 'A boy. My baby was a boy.'

'Did you ever wonder if he'd coming looking for you?' I said, earning an alarmed glance from Esme. 'In the same way that I'm looking for my mother, now?'

A wistful smile formed at the corner of Cindy's mouth. 'That'd be a lovely thought,' she said. 'But it ain't gonna happen.' She pushed away her coffee. 'My baby died a couple of minutes after he was born.'

27

'Should we have told her the truth?' I said, as I watched Cindy Walker leave the cafe. She picked up a wire basket and disappeared between the aisles of the supermarket.

'There may well come a time for her to know what really happened,' Esme said. 'But this is hardly the place. Besides, it would be far better coming from someone used to dealing with a situation like this. A counsellor.'

I tried to imagine how it would be to learn that your baby survived, only to find he'd been killed in a road accident before you got the chance to meet. How could you deal with that?

I looked round at Esme. Something in her eyes worried me. I sensed she understood more about what Cindy had told us than I did? 'How did it happen?' I asked her. 'Why did she think Matthew had died?'

'Because that's what she was told.'

'Yeah, but why?'

'Because if the mother thinks her baby is dead, there's no danger of her searching for him or her at some point in the future.'

'And turning up unannounced on Mr and Mrs Collins's doorstep, or any of the other parents involved in the sordid scheme.'

'If the adoption was through legal channels, the mother knows that she has no rights to make contact with her baby, that it's for the child to decide when he or she reaches the age of eighteen. All she can do is let it be known that she's willing to be contacted. But in this scenario there are no rules.'

Something terrifying began stirring in my head but I pushed it away. I wasn't ready to face it yet. 'Do you think Mr and Mrs Collins knew that's how it worked?'

'I doubt it. They would have assumed, I'm sure, that Matthew's birth mother had agreed to the adoption.' Esme slid her coffee cup to one side and rested her elbows on the table. 'This has echoes of a scandal that blew up in Spain a few years ago.'

I frowned. 'What scandal?'

'That, over a period of about fifty years, unmarried mothers in the care of the Church were told that their newborn babies had died in childbirth. The Church went to extraordinary lengths to enforce the myth, even going so far as conducting funerals and burials. But it was all lies. The babies weren't dead at all. They were sold to wealthy childless couples.'

'Sold?'

Esme nodded. 'I'm afraid so.'

I forced myself to ask the question even though I already knew the answer. 'That's what Monsell and Jarrett were doing, isn't it? Selling those poor girls' babies.' I tapped my chest 'They sold me, like I was just a commodity.'

'We don't know that for certain – we only have Cindy's evidence to go by so far. Interestingly, in Spain, the law protected the anonymity of an unmarried mother by allowing the term "mother unknown" to be recorded when registering a birth. Here, of course, while there's no obligation to record the name of the father, the mother does have to be named.'

'Which is why my birth certificate's a fabrication.' I blinked away tears and swallowed. 'Fifty years.' I shook my head. 'It's horrible. How many babies? How many mothers lied to?' I thought of Cindy, the shadow in her eyes as she told us about the death of her baby. And I thought of my own birth mother being told the same. I must find her. I must let her know it wasn't true.

Esme reached for my hand and squeezed it. 'Come on. We've work to do.'

'Yes,' I said, wiping a tear from my cheek. 'We have. But where do we go from here? Cindy was a victim. She's not told us anything to move us forward.'

'Yes she has – the cellar. There was no mention of it in the sales particulars.'

I recalled Esme standing at the back of the building, trying to work something out, moments before the old lady caused a stir. 'You said something didn't match up.'

'Nor did it. I think the cellar had been bricked up.'

A shiver ran down my back. 'To hide something?'

'Why else would you do it?' Esme tipped her head to one side and looked at me with concern. 'If you're up to it, I think it's time to pay another visit to Devon.'

28

As we travelled down the M5, Esme filled me in with what she hoped to establish on our visit.

'The record office are going to dig out the original plans of Hawks Hall for me. From them I can confirm whether there was a cellar and whether it had an entrance like the one Cindy mentioned. There was certainly nothing obvious so, assuming it did exist, whoever blocked it up did a professional job.'

'Maybe we can find out who the builder was? He may have seen what was down there.'

'If there was anything to hide, I'm pretty sure Madam Matron would have made certain he didn't get sight of it.'

'Unless she paid him off.'

'It's a thought.'

As we sailed past Bristol, I began to get nervous. Were we on the brink of revealing the final chapter of what had dominated my brain for the past month or would our trail disappear in the dense Exmoor drizzle?

*

'Are you sure you want to do this?' Esme asked, as we stood gazing across the fields on the edge of Westford.

I stared over the style to where hundreds of feet had flattened the grass along the hedge line. 'That's the footpath that girl took when she ran away from the hall, isn't it?'

'I think so. I'd love to know what happened to her. I wonder if she ever reported anything about what she thought was going on.'

'I doubt anyone would have taken her seriously if she had,' I said, shoving my hands deep in my jacket pockets. 'Once she finally got away she probably decided to stay well out of it.' I gave Esme a wry smile. 'Hey, maybe she was my real mum? Wouldn't that be cool?'

Esme smiled back, happy to indulge in my fantasy. 'Whoever she was, she did a greater job than she realised. As the old lady said, it was probably because of her that Marilyn Jarrett panicked and shut the place down.'

'What we don't know, of course,' I said as the horrible thought struck me, 'is whether she set up somewhere else.'

'I somehow doubt it,' Esme said. 'It must have made her wary. And that's assuming she'd have the capital. As far as we know, she still owns Hawks Hall.'

'So why sell it now?'

Esme nodded. 'Exactly what I thought. Perhaps someone forced her hand.' She pulled her car keys out of her pocket. 'Well, I'd better get off to the record office.'

'Couldn't they just scan the plans and email them to you?'

Esme gave me a patient look. 'We're talking original blueprints,' she said, spreading her hands wide. 'Even if they had a suitable size scanner, it'd be a couple of days before they could get to it. Easier if I nip in and have a look at it myself. I can copy the relevant section if I think it's worth it.' She paused. 'You can come with me, if you like?'

'No, it's fine. I'd rather have a chat to the woman in the B & B. See if she's got any more to add to what she told Mick.' I nodded towards the pub. 'Besides, I asked the barmaid to put the word around that if anyone remembered anything about Hawks Hall, to give me a call. I thought I'd drop in the pub at lunchtime too.'

Esme buttoned up her coat. 'Well, let me know. I'll be as quick as I can. If I find out anything useful, we might have time for a look-see later before we head back.'

I nodded. 'OK. I'll give you a call when I've seen Mrs B & B. Let you know what she said.'

'Right. Better text me in case I'm in the record office.'

'Oh, yeah, right.' I grinned. 'I forget all this protocol.'

Esme strode across the square to her car and I headed in the direction as instructed, looking for a stone house with bay windows and a large front garden. I found it in less than five minutes. There was a low iron gate on to a path leading directly to the front door. The gate opened with a satisfying squeak and I made my way up to the front door. An old-fashioned bell-pull hung on the front wall to one side. It appeared rusty and hardly likely to do the job but I gave it a yank anyway and was surprised to hear a distant jangle from inside.

A smartly dressed elderly lady with grey hair cut neatly looked out at me with friendly curiosity. 'Yes?' she said. 'Can I help?'

I introduced myself, saying I was doing some family-history research and had been born near here. We'd debated whether to mention Mick Sheldon but, having no idea if he'd been received favourably, I was wary of shooting myself in the foot before I started.

The lady gave me an indulgent smile. 'I'm sorry, I'm not sure I fully understand. Are you saying your family has links with this house?'

'Possibly,' I said, thinking on my feet. 'My late mother mentioned staying here.' I cleared my throat and jumped in. 'I was born at a maternity home not far from here.'

She blinked. 'Oh, I see.'

'I've been trying to find out more about the home. It was called –'

'Hawks Hall. Yes, I know the one you mean.' Her brow puckered. 'Are you related to Mr and Mrs Collins?'

'Not related, no, but I do know them. Mr Collins, anyway,' I added hastily. While I might be stretching a point, I didn't want to set myself up to fall into any traps. 'They stayed with you, I believe, when...when Matthew was born.' I gave her a broad smile.

'I'm sorry, Miss Vincent –'

'Gina.'

'Gina. But I'm confused as to how I can help. I've had many guests over the years. If you're asking if I remember if your mother stayed –'

'No, of course not. I wouldn't expect you to. I just wondered what do you remember about Hawks Hall.'

'Nothing, my dear. I've never been.'

'A girl ran away from the hall a short time before the home closed and was found wandering the village. Do you remember anything about that?'

She frowned. 'No, I'm afraid I don't. I do recall the story but I was away from home at the time. Now, I really have things to do. I'm sorry I can't be more help.' She began to close the door.

'Are you sure there isn't anything else you can remember? What about when the Collinses stayed?'

'I wish you success in your enquiries, my dear. But I'm afraid I've nothing more to say. Goodbye.'

I stood, staring at the closed door. Was she hiding something or was I just a hopeless investigator? Had I said something to alarm her? I sighed. She didn't appear alarmed. Her insistence that she had nothing to add seemed genuine enough. How would Esme have fared? Would she have made more progress? Perhaps I should have gone to the record office and left Esme to do the visit.

I turned and retreated down the path as my phone rang. I pulled it out of my pocket and looked at the screen. It was a number I didn't recognise. I put the phone to my ear. 'Gina Vincent.'

'Ah, Gina,' said a woman's voice. 'My name's Grace O'Brien. I believe you're interested in Hawks Hall?'

'Yes, that's right. Do you have some information?'

The woman chuckled. 'You could say. I worked at the hall for several years as a cook.'

'That's brilliant,' I said, with a thrill of anticipation. 'Where could we meet?'

'Let me think. I could see you at the pub, if you like... No, wait a minute. Even better. Why don't I meet you at Hawks Hall? It'd be fun to see the old place again.'

I was about to say I couldn't, that I had no transport, but then remembered the footpath the runaway girl had taken. Meeting someone there who knew the place well could prove very useful. She might even know how to access the cellar. 'OK,' I said, imagining my call to Esme telling her I'd solved the mystery on the ground, instead of studying dusty blueprints. 'What time?'

'Shall we say in about half an hour?'

That should give me enough time to walk there. 'Great. Half an hour it is, then.'

'Lovely, my dear. Look forward to it.'

29

I texted Esme to bring her up to date and headed out of the village. The public footpath pointed over a style. I climbed over it and took the path across the fields to where Hawks Hall lay a mile and a half away on the edge of the moor. There was a dampness in the air and I hoped that wasn't a sign of rain to come – my denim jacket wasn't designed to withstand the onslaught of inclement moorland weather.

On the other side of the field, the footpath came out on to a narrow bridleway, enclosed on either side by ancient drystone banks sprouting with vegetation and stunted shrubby growth on the top. I hurried along, avoiding the worst of the mud as best I could and wishing that when I'd agreed to meet Grace I'd given some thought to my footwear, which was proving inadequate for a country walk.

I was relieved when the track opened out into a metalled lane and I could see the chimneys of Hawks Hall in the distance. It was a different approach from the time we'd come as pseudo punters to the viewing open day. From this position, I could almost believe that the place was alive and inhabited. I imagined it being bought by a family who'd raise chickens in the yard at the back, climb trees on the boundaries and run up to a high point to fly kites in the wind which blew across the moorland landscape.

But as I rounded the corner my fantasy was shattered and I saw again the forlorn building with its faded paintwork and broken windows. I stopped and stood in the eerie silence. What traumas had the abandoned structure witnessed? What secrets could it spill?

I gave myself a mental shake and strode into the overgrown yard. Grace hadn't yet arrived. At least, no car was parked there, or in the lane beyond the gate. Perhaps she'd walked, like me. But there was no sign of anyone. I checked the time. I was early. I may as well take the opportunity to look around for signs of the hidden cellar entrance.

It must be around the back. You'd hardly put such a lowly access on the front facade. Unless that was the trick of it. Who'd think to look there? But a quick walk around didn't give me any suggestions that the architect had been that innovative so I headed round to the rear and slowed my pace so I could peer more closely into the bays and crevices of the adjoining structures of walls, steps and terraces.

If I'd been a casual observer, I wouldn't have spotted it but, as my focus was concentrated, it was relatively easy to make out. Halfway up a flight of shallow steps, I paused to look down into the narrow void between the rising side wall of the staircase and that of the house. Below me, in a dark corner, I could make out some sort of recess.

I ran down the steps and squeezed my way down the slim passage. In the recess was a narrow door but it didn't match the faded, peeling paint of the remainder of the house's decoration. It was brighter, as though it had been protected from the elements. As I stepped closer, I realised that's exactly what had happened. Under my feet were pieces of broken planking. Until very recently, this doorway had been covered by a decorative panel and disguised. So who had uncovered it? It couldn't have been there at the viewing.

I thought of Esme and wondered how she was getting on. She needed to know about this. I pulled out my phone and checked my messages. But there was nothing from Esme. Only the icon to tell me I had no mobile service, which I guessed would have been the same for most of my walk from the village.

I shoved the phone back into my pocket and stepped closer to the door. I pushed it but it didn't give. About halfway down was a tiny metal knob. It was so corroded I wasn't convinced it would turn. Perhaps whoever had taken off the panelling had made no more progress than this. It looked as though the door hadn't been opened in decades.

I grasped the knob and turned it, wincing at the grating noise which set my teeth on edge. I braced myself and pushed. Another shove with my shoulder and the door gave way. I stumbled inside.

I could almost taste the stench of damp but, surprisingly, the room wasn't completely dark. A series of grilles above allowed in a modicum of light. Even so, it still took a few moments for my eyes to adjust. Once they had, I gazed around the room, taking in the grubby white walls, caked with distemper, invading strands of ivy and blackened cobwebs hanging from the low ceiling. On the far wall to my left was a half-opened door, which I guessed was where the cellar was accessed from within the house, where steps led to the floor above. To my right was another door, closed and – strangely, it seemed to me – barred with a rusty padlock. A pile of assorted furniture was piled unceremoniously against the far wall.

I blinked into the gloom. Had this been the delivery room which Cindy mentioned? My innards lurched. If it was, then this was the room where I was born. I stepped further inside. In the far corner, hidden from view until now by the half open door was a dark grey metal filing cabinet, thick with dust and cobwebs dotted with the bodies of dead flies. No, not the delivery room. This must have been an office. Matron's lair, as Cindy had called it.

An image of the photos of the files Matthew Collins had taken with his phone came into my head. Was it possible that the files in here were those which would give me the information I craved?

I strode over to the cabinet and yanked at the top drawer. Locked. I gave the cabinet a kick of frustration. At the same time, it gave me hope. Who'd lock an empty filing cabinet? There must be something of value inside. I looked around for something to smash the lock but saw nothing. Perhaps a rock from outside.

I turned to retrace my steps, when the silhouetted figure of a woman appeared in the doorway.

I recoiled, slapping the flat of my hand against my chest. 'Oh, Grace. Hi.' I'd almost forgotten about our meeting. 'Thanks for coming.'

'Hello, Gina,' she said. 'We meet again.'

'Again?' I frowned. 'Sorry – have we met before?'

'Yes, dear. At the very moment you came into this world.'

'What?' I didn't understand. Why would the cook be present at my birth?

Grace stepped into the dim light and for the first time I saw her face. A face I'd seen before. It was the woman in Mick Sheldon's photograph. The woman who called herself Harriet Monsell.

30

For a moment all I could do was stare. Her appearance had altered little. She still wore a bandanna around her head and the same wisps of hair escaped from it. Except the hair was grey now, the face had grown puffy and sagged around the mouth. The eyes, however, remained as sharp and angry as before.

My gaze fell upon a large book she held against her. An old-fashioned ledger.

'You're Marilyn Jarrett,' I said, pointlessly.

She moved closer. Instinctively, I backed away.

'I know what you want,' she said. 'But you shan't have it. That wasn't the idea at all.' She walked over to the filing cabinet and pulled out a set of keys from her pocket.

I swallowed. 'What is it you think I want?'

'After everything I did to protect you.' Her voice was so low, she could have almost been talking to herself. She slid a key into the lock on the cabinet and turned it.

'Protect me?' I stepped a little closer. 'Protect me from what, for God's sake?'

She pulled open the drawer and dropped the ledger inside, before reeling round. 'You stupid girl.' No low tones now. 'How can you not see?' She spoke as though dealing with a wayward child who failed to understand the consequences of their actions. 'I freed them. They don't need their past coming back to haunt them. The slate has been wiped clean. Their sins are forgiven. They can go back out into the world unburdened.'

I glared at her. The woman was clearly unhinged. My overwhelming instinct was to leave, to get as far away as possible from this surreal scene and this distasteful woman. But the filing cabinet was only feet away. Inside could be everything I needed to know. And more besides – the truth for dozens of others in the same situation as me. But Marilyn Jarrett stood between me and my salvation.

'You told them their babies were dead, didn't you?' I said with more bravado than I felt.

She gave a dismissive shake of the head. 'So?'

'But those mothers grieved a lie. How could you do that?'

'The babies did not suffer. They were taken in by parents who loved them, who –'

'Who *paid* for them. And went on paying, too.' I was shaking now. 'For how long, eh? Until they reached adulthood? Until they moved out of the family home? Until their death?'

'No, no. You're quite wrong.' She pulled herself up to

her full height. 'I did not sanction greed.'

'But you sold those babies. You sold me!'

'Only to fund the service.'

'Service? Call it a service, denying people the knowledge of their true parentage?'

She stabbed a finger in the air. 'I gave the gift of parenthood to those who could not do so naturally. In return they made a payment towards the running of Hawks Hall. That is all.' She took a step towards me. 'How dare you lecture me? What sort of twisted world is it when young girls who can barely wipe their own noses are expected to become mothers at so young an age? And why should innocent babies have their lives blighted by misguided liberal thinking that no matter what depraved lives their mothers live they should be allowed to keep their wretched child?' She cocked her chin. 'I saved those children. And I saved their mothers. It was an act of mercy.'

"Didn't see eye to eye on policy", Evelyn Lloyd had said. So, Marilyn Jarrett had decided to do things her own way, had she?

'What happened to the girl who tried to run away?' I said. 'Did you save her too?'

The woman's face grew dark. She snorted. 'Disobedient, subversive child. She spoiled everything. When the press turned up I knew it was over. I wasn't prepared to wait around while they spouted flawed sanctimonious objections to my scheme and destroyed all the good work I'd achieved.'

'So you closed down.' Ironic that Mick Sheldon's boss wasn't interested in pursuing the story. How many more lives would she have affected if she'd known she'd got away with it? 'And when you couldn't make money selling babies you resorted to blackmail instead.'

'No, I did not!' she said. 'That was not my doing. Lance... he didn't understand. I tried to tell him but he wouldn't listen. Wouldn't see the harm. We argued. He... We...'

Something clicked. 'He left you,' I said, my eye falling on the filing cabinet. 'And took that ledger with him.'

'The fool. I should have guessed when I realised one of the books was missing. And then that *boy*...' She almost spat the word.

'Boy?'

'But it was too late by then. The Collins boy had got what he wanted.'

'Matthew,' I said, irritated. 'His name was Matthew. And all he wanted to know – like I do, and I'd guess all of us who are affected by your sordid scheme want to know – the identity of our mothers.'

She turned back to the cabinet. She closed the top drawer and opened the bottom one, from where she lifted out a container. Even before the smell of petrol reached my nostrils I realised what she intended to do.

'No!' I lurched forward, pulling her away from the cabinet and kicking the lower drawer closed. She came at me. I stuck out my elbow, trying to open the top drawer at the same time. It was hopeless. There was no way I could find what I wanted while she set a fire to destroy everything. I had to stop her.

I made a grab for the container but she dodged and I stumbled. I felt a pain in my head and everything went black.

31

I came to, immediately aware of the smell of smoke. I lifted my head off the hard stone floor, wincing as it pounded like the world's worst hangover, and sat up. There was no sign of Marilyn Jarrett and in the limited light I could see enough to know that I didn't have long to get out. The mismatched heap of furniture smouldered across the room, chair legs sticking out at grotesque angles, like a livestock funeral pyre during a Foot and Mouth outbreak. Already the light above was being supplemented by the orange glow of flames licking at its centre. I guessed I could thank the damp upholstery for slowing down the fire taking hold, but it only increased the smoke.

I pushed myself on to my feet, a spasm of coughing overwhelming me as I came into contact with the thicker fumes. I grabbed the corner of my jacket, stuffing it across my nose and mouth and dropped back down to the floor. My naive plan that I could somehow retrieve what I needed from those metal drawers before making my escape showed itself to be the insane idea that it was. Marilyn

Jarrett had got her way. No evidence would remain of the young women whose babies the Jarretts had sold. There would be no joyous reunions, no wrongs righted, no questions of birth answered.

But I wasn't ready to give in yet. Maybe there was time for one last try.

Keeping my face low, I dragged myself across to the filing cabinet. The top drawer was open. I pulled myself up and peered inside. Nothing. The drawer was empty. She'd taken everything. I sank to the floor, defeated.

It was then that I saw the torn pages on the floor. She would have realised the books wouldn't burn whole and had ripped them apart to be more easily consumed by the fire. But in her haste she had dropped some sheets and several lay within reach on the floor. There was still a chance to salvage something.

I used one hand to press my jacket to my face to filter the flames and with the other, in a spasm of coughing, grabbed the page closest to me, scrambling on my knees for another and another until the smoke engulfed me and my eyes were stinging. As I dragged myself across the floor, the hopelessness of my task overwhelmed me. I didn't have time for this. I had to get out now or I'd die in the attempt. And what good would that do? I clutched the pages against me and stumbled towards the door, falling against it with relief. I grabbed the handle and turned. Nothing happened. The door remained stubbornly shut.

The papers slipped from my arms and I threw myself at the door, first lunging at it with my shoulder and then kicking it, yelling at it to give way. With my energy spent, I sank down to the ground, pressing my face against the marginal crack at the foot of the door, gasping at the trickle of air filtering through from outside.

The encounter with Marilyn Jarrett replayed in my head. This time I watched myself from a distance. This time I was more forceful in my arguments. She saw the error of her ways. She cowed as I demanded my details. She handed over a book. I looked at a page. I saw a name. I smiled. I floated in a haze of white mist. All was calm. Quiet.

There was a crash. The floating turned violent. I was knocked backwards, then dragged. I tried to resist, my arms flailing at my attackers. Voices cried out for me to stop. And then cutting through all the rest, a voice I knew. Esme's. And I knew I was safe.

32

The blackened wall where the fire had been didn't improve Hawks Hall's decrepit appearance. As I stood in the yard looking across at the forlorn structure, draped in the remains of blue and white police tape, I wondered if an input of TLC and some imagination by a new owner could wipe away the residue of heartlessness which I fancied lurked in the fabric of the building.

I walked across the courtyard and placed my modest posy of primroses against the wall of the house – my heartfelt, if inadequate, tribute to the unknown runaway girl, whose remains had been found in the fire-damaged building.

I turned at the sound of a car, watching as Esme pulled into the yard and climbed out of her car.

'How was your walk from the village?' she said as she joined me. 'As therapeutic as you'd hoped?'

I thrust my hands deep into my coat pockets. 'Didn't feel anything much. No overwhelming desire to run in the opposite direction, anyway. So I guess that's good, right?'

'I'd say so.'

I turned back to the house and we stood, gazing in silence.

'God, Esme. What would have happened to me if I hadn't texted you that woman's name?' I shuddered. 'I'd be dead.'

'"What if" is the most indefensible phrase in the English language. "What if" I'd not read your text until much later? "What if" I hadn't known that the real Harriet Monsell had an unmarried sister called Grace O'Brien? But we did. You did. It happened and we survived and Marilyn Jarrett's been charged with murder.'

My eye was drawn back to the charred wall and I felt the sting of tears. 'Hard to think of that poor girl being only a few feet away from me all the time I was there.'

'You weren't to know.'

'Well, we should have known. We should have taken more notice of Cindy Walker. "Locking us up without our dinner was more her style", she told us. And that they didn't go down to the cellar unless they broke the rules.'

'Which, as far as Marilyn Jarrett was concerned, was exactly what our runaway did.'

'"Disobedient and subversive" were her exact words,' I said, recalling the rage I'd seen on her face. 'Did she mean to leave her down there, d'you think? Or did she genuinely forget about her in her panic to get away?'

Esme closed her eyes and shook her head with a shudder.

'She couldn't have left as quickly as all that. It would have taken a few days to organise for the rest of the girls to leave. But I wouldn't be surprised if she was the only one who knew the girl was down there. Lance Jarrett couldn't have known or he wouldn't have arranged the place going up for sale.'

I hugged myself. 'Why the hell didn't it occur to me to ask, why come all the way back here to get rid of a few ledger books? She could have done that anywhere. I should have realised she had more to hide. That poor girl. All I was bothered about was bloody paperwork.'

'Don't be too hard on yourself, Gina. That paperwork will go a long way to getting justice for her, once they track down everyone in the pages you salvaged.'

'She was some gutsy girl. Without her we'd have never uncovered the truth. And we don't even know her name.'

Esme put her arm around my shoulders. 'There's still time.'

'Why was she never missed, d'you think?'

'Dysfunctional family, perhaps? Everyone assumes she's gone off of her own accord. Even if anyone asked questions, they may not be on the ball enough to push the point.'

I sighed. 'Bounced from one dysfunctional situation to another, poor maid.'

'Picking up the local lingo, I see?' Esme teased.

'Sure.' I said, with a weak smile. 'I'm a Devon-born girl, remember?'

Esme smiled briefly before her face took on a more serious expression. 'Nervous?'

I shook myself. 'Don't want to think about it. Not yet.' I cleared my throat. 'So tell me about something else. What's the latest?'

'Well,' Esme said, tipping her head to one side and considering, 'let me think. Nothing official but, from what Collins has said, Lance Jarrett was already milking the system before the place closed down. He'd already hiked up the fee she charged and was creaming off the excess.'

'She said something about her not sanctioning greed. Guess she found out about that.'

'That fertility clinic has a few questions to answer. Someone on the staff seems to have given people like the Collinses the information about Hawks Hall. Oh, and Mick Sheldon's talking about writing a book.'

'His long-awaited exclusive not enough, then?'

'Oh, I don't think it's that. He was as thrilled as I was that so many came forward after reading it.' I could feel her eyes on me. 'Particularly in your case.'

I stared into the middle distance, seeing those disgorged books on the floor and experiencing a sense of panic that I'd never be able to save them. 'You can't imagine how horrible I felt when my name wasn't on those pages. It seemed like the end of the world. That I'd lost the last chance to ever find out.' I looked round at Esme. 'I didn't even think about DNA tests. How stupid's that?'

'Any mother remembers the birth date of her baby. From there it's easy.' Esme checked her watch. 'Come on, you. Or we'll be late.'

We drove back to the village, both lost in our private thoughts. Esme was right, of course. No point in dwelling on what might have happened. In the end, we achieved everything we could have expected to do. I'd been lucky, and if Mick Sheldon did write his book, it might flush out others who currently lived with uncertainty and with no obvious way to resolve their situation.

Esme pulled up in the square and turned off the engine. I looked across to the pub and the nervousness gripped me once more. 'What if she doesn't like me? What if we don't get on?'

Esme reached over and patted my hand. 'There you go again. "What if? What if?"'

I gave a half-hearted laugh. 'Sorry,' I said, holding my hands up in mock surrender. 'Panic over.'

'Glad to hear it. Now, off you go.'

I opened the car door and climbed out, pausing to lean back inside. 'Thanks, Esme. Thanks for everything.'

Esme smiled. 'You're very welcome. Now stop stalling. She'll be wondering where you are. And remember,' she leaned across to the central console and peered up at me, 'she'll be just as nervous.'

I nodded and slammed the door shut, before taking a deep breath and striding off towards the pub. At the edge of the path I slowed to glance over my shoulder to watch as Esme drove away.

I never did find out her story. Where had she got her scar? What happened in her past which had gave her the empathy for my situation? I frowned. I must ask her sometime. Meanwhile, there were other things on my mind.

I stood up straight and marched up the path to meet my mother.

Thank you for reading *Death of a Cuckoo*. If you enjoyed the book and have a moment to spare, writing a short review on your favourite site would be greatly appreciated. Authors rely on the kindness of readers to spread the word.

To sign up for updates on giveaways, special promotions and new releases, please sign up for my newsletter on my website: www.wendypercival.co.uk.

You can also visit me on Facebook:
www.facebook.com/wendypercivalauthor
and on Twitter: @wendy_percival

I look forward to hearing from you.

Lightning Source UK Ltd.
Milton Keynes UK
UKHW010755310821
389774UK00002B/229